THE
Challenge

Wendy Everts

Stonebrook Publishing
Saint Louis, Missouri

A STONEBROOK PUBLISHING BOOK

Edited by Nancy L. Erickson, The Book Professor
TheBookProfessor.com

Scripture quotations are from the
ESV® Bible (*The Holy Bible, English Standard Version*®),
copyright © 2001 by Crossway,
a publishing ministry of Good News Publishers.
Used by permission. All rights reserved.

Library of Congress Control Number: 2016939011
ISBN: 978-0-9975210-0-9

www.stonebrookpublishing.net

PRINTED IN THE UNITED STATES OF AMERICA
10 9 8 7 6 5 4 3 2 1

I couldn't wait to hear the ending, but then I didn't want it to be over! I think about the characters all the time.

Andrea Schrieber, twelve years old

Finally! A gripping, fascinating book for any teenage girl! As a ministry director, I am always looking for relatable, well-written Christian books that I can passionately endorse. This fits the bill. You won't be disappointed.

Trish Helsel, Executive Women's Director of Kanakuk Ministries

Wendy Everts is a master communicator and has the knack for presenting issues of faith and life in real-world terms through real-life settings. *The Challenge* is a strong work packaged in a story for middle-school girls that can strengthen their relationship with their peers, their families, and with Jesus Christ. I highly recommend it!

Dr. Tom Hill, author of Blessed Beyond Measure, Living at the Summit, and Chicken Soup for the Entrepreneur's Soul

In *The Challenge*, we are given a beautiful gift: truth wrapped up in story. I'm amazed at how my family was simultaneously enthralled (it's a great story!) and changed (these are powerful discipleship principles!).

Rev. Don Everts, author of thirteen books including Jesus With Dirty Feet and Go & Do: Becoming a Missional Christian

I love Clover and her family's brokenness because it is so relatable. We all want to stop spinning and set our feet heartily on God's path. In steps the hero, God, who reveals Himself through the wealthy Mrs. Belle, Clover's gifted friends and her secretive mom. I finished this book and was reminded to pray that God would line up harvest workers to pour God's love and grace into my own children.

DeAnn Feltz, mother of three

As I've searched for discipleship resources that shape the emerging identities of adolescent girls, I've struggled to find many that are equally enjoyed by both mature adults and young teens. Wendy has written an engaging novel that is full of ideas for bridging the cultural divide between young women and the adults who yearn to understand and minister to them. *The Challenge* provides an amazing springboard for deep discussions that matter as tweens, teens and adults explore how Christ's love for them impacts the way they navigate this crazy world. I'm looking forward to reading it with my 8th grade discipleship group this year!

Shannon Hathaway, 8th grade discipleship leader

The Challenge invites scripture to come alive in a way that is tangible and needed for this generation. Not only does it speak to young people, but it also walks those of any age through the meaning of believing in someone younger than them.

David Paterka, founder of "When the Saints" ministry

In *The Challenge*, teens will meet a friend who struggles honestly with questions about friendship, family dynamics, and faith. The struggle is real and the message is clear: life can be hard and confusing, but it does not have to be lived alone and in the dark. Clover and her family show teens and adults alike how to step into the light and how to bring people with them.

Sarah K. Macky, middle school teacher

Even as a twenty-year-old male college student, I was surprised at how much I related to the characters. This book reminded me that there are struggles in finding Christ, but He meets us where we are. I loved how the main character changed in seeing people differently and brought more life to her relationships.

Tim Whyman, student and videographer

After going to a mother/daughter retreat using this book, I wanted to have one of my own. I have a list of moms and daughters ready to go. Not sure where or when ... but I can't stop thinking about it!

Abbey Francis, mother of two daughters

For more information about using *The Challenge* for small groups, retreats, book clubs, and family discussion, please go to www.orderthechallenge.com. Leader and Discussion Guides are available free for download.

THE
Challenge

Wendy Everts

I dedicate this book to my daughter who was thirteen not so long ago. My heart will always be open to you. Let's never lock our doors.

Matthew 6:21

For where your treasure is,
there your heart will be also.

Dear Diary

Sometimes I feel like a potato in a sack of french fries. No one has ever said, "What I really want right now is a plain and boring potato with nothing on it." No. They go for the french fries. They talk about them. They argue about which restaurant has the best ones. Even if people don't eat french fries, they want them. They crave them. They make a choice not to eat them.

I guess I am still waiting to be made into something special. To be something that is wanted. Talked about. Noticed. How does that happen? How can I be transformed into something different? How do I be what people want? If I knew, I would do it right now. I can't stand that achy, lonely, nothing feeling in my chest.

Until then, I will pretend that I feel special like everyone else. I will act like a french fry in a middle school that's full of other french fries.

~Clover Mannerhouse

The Move

$\mathcal{W}$e moved to the small town of Hitlery, California, just last summer, one year ago. Can you believe that name? When my dad announced that we were moving out of Los Angeles, I was against it.

My dad's background was in marketing, and he did commercials and voice-overs for bad lawyer ads. On the days I was sick and stayed home from school, my mom would turn on the TV and watch soap operas. Evidently that was prime time for bad lawyer ads. My dad's snarky voice would blare, "Have you been injured in a car accident? Call Mally and Beane Associates. We can help you get the money you deserve! Don't wait; call now. We are on your team!"

My parents were tired of barely making ends meet, so my dad was always looking for a better job. He found a shopping network in the small town of Hitlery, California, of all places. It was the perfect job for him. His smooth-talking voice, combined with the fact that he could chat for a long time about one thing, made him a shoe-in for the job. In the interview they gave him a rubber duck and put him in front of the camera for five minutes to see if he could sell it. At the end of two minutes, they turned the cameras off and offered him the job on the spot.

It was a miserable day when he sat my brother and me down to sell us on the move. His voice was fake and nervous. "Kids, I want to tell you about a great opportunity we have as a family! Picture this … a city with a population of 100,000 rather than three million. Imagine going to a grocery store and bumping into someone you know. Think of a city where there are people just like us!"

We stared at him with squinty looks and tried to understand his presentation. "Can you not use your lawyer-ad voice please, and just talk to us?" I asked.

Ryan was older than me and put it together more quickly, "Yeah, we aren't on the shopping network. We are your kids. I know what's going on. We are either going on vacation or moving. Gosh darn it! Tell me we aren't moving!" That was my brother's way of swearing. My parents weren't pious people, but one thing they didn't tolerate was swearing.

"It's funny you should mention the shopping network," my dad said under his breath. Then he looked at us real stern. "Don't think of it as moving; think of it as a much needed fresh start."

It was time for me to get serious, "For you or us, Dad? Unlike you and Mom, we have friends here, and there is not a place on this green earth where there are people like us. Mom wears a different gaudy wig every day and puts on high heels just to go to the Laundromat, like she is one of those moms who is trying to be younger than she really is. She smacks her gum and has a quirky hand motion for every word she says!"

When my mother, Maggie Ann Mannerhouse, said the word "together," she pronounced it "toogethah" and touched her pointer fingers together like they were meeting for coffee.

My dad continued to defend his view that we really were, in fact, a normal family, while I daydreamed about all the memories that proved him wrong. I was used to daydreaming while he went on and on about things.

I didn't want to move, but I also found humor in imagining ourselves pulling up to a new neighborhood and seeing how a small community would respond to us. By "us" I really meant my mom. I didn't realize how embarrassing she was until I was old enough to be interested in reading magazines about how to give yourself a fake tan. One article described how to do a believable job that left you with golden skin and how to do a bad job that gave you orange skin. My mom was orange.

One time we went to the store, and she picked up a magazine that had movie stars with bad fake tans on the cover. She smacked her gum and read the article, her orange face absorbed by the words. I felt like the magazine was making fun of her too. I couldn't stand it. "We live in California, Mom, there is NO reason for a bad fake tan. Geeeez!!!!!" I said.

She put the magazine down and started blinking a lot. Then she suddenly remembered that she forgot something in aisle three and ran off. She did that a lot. I never saw her cry, but she certainly walked away from me like she was about to all the time.

People often asked me where my mom grew up, and my favorite answer was, "She was born in the State of Confusion." After laughing, they usually guessed based on the way she talked. I had to warn them, "Don't try to figure it out from her accent. She doesn't have one. She speaks *Maggie Ann*." When I didn't give a straight answer, they were convinced from her obvious fake wigs that she grew up right there in California. Others were SURE she was from Jersey. I created a ridiculous story and said she was from a small ranch in Montana, where she lived off the land, shot her own food, and tanned hides to make her own clothes. If they continued to hound me for details, I did what all typical thirteen-year-old girls without manners did. I said, "Ask her yourself." My mom hated to talk about her past, so why should I be the one to tell them?

My mom had a very special way of getting us to do our chores. If we didn't fold our laundry when she asked, she talked loudly to herself, "Hmmmm. Now … where IS my very special black marker that never washes out! I think this pink blouse would look lovely with a big smiley face right on the front! Wait … isn't this YOUR pink blouse, Clovah?" My name is Clover, but my mom said it with a special Maggie Ann mouth. It was like she had a child's speech impediment that never went away.

If we didn't empty the dishwasher immediately, she actually dropped the dishes "accidentally" on the floor to break them. "Oh my goodness my hands are so slippery. I just don't know what we'll eat off of if I keep dropping all these dishes! And we can't afford any more even if we go to the thrift store!" Not only did we have to finish putting the dishes away, we had to clean up the broken ones.

Perhaps my favorite Maggie Ann tradition—and by favorite I mean that I hated it—happened during Christmas. Every year she spent hours and hours making me a very special Christmas ornament. That doesn't sound so terrible, but it always symbolized a boy from my class. It started in grade school when she volunteered as Room Mom, or as I like to call it, Classroom Spy.

The first time she gave me one of her ornaments, I was blindsided. I was in second grade, and I loved a boy named Barrett Barrow. It was an innocent second grade crush. In my mom's eyes, I was as good as married to the boy. During the afternoons while my brother and I were in school, Maggie Ann made the most intricate wheelbarrow out of paper clips with a wire bender. She turned on the TV and added to her creation every afternoon. She painted it red, and then made clay figurines of me and Barrett Barrow to put in the wheelbarrow.

On Christmas Eve when little children all over the world opened gifts of cozy new pajamas, I opened my first ornament and saw what was obviously me and a boy sitting in the wheelbarrow, holding hands. Maggie Ann said, "It's you and that little

Barrett boy who's in your class Clovah! Toogethah!" Pointer fingers right on cue.

"I wanted pajamas like everyone else! This is weird Mom," I said. Second graders are good at telling their moms what they think. She took the ornament and put it on the tree. I remember having an *aha!* moment when she hung it on the branch. Until then, I hadn't realized that it was an ornament. I didn't understand any of it, really.

The next year, I got a very ornate cross-stitched "R" on a tiny piece of linen that she made into a round ornament. There were a bunch of little snail shells glued on the wreath-like circle around the R. I said, "Let me guess, Ronnie Shell?" and my very proud mother squealed, "Yes! Yes! Clovah, he is such a fine boy and I'm so glad you two have become friends." I wouldn't even say we were friends. I sat by him in class. My mom was crazy.

In fourth grade, I got what I thought was a huge bag of popcorn. It turned out to be a popcorn garland for the tree. A very long one.

"I've seen the way you look at that boy Byron Garland, sweetie! He's a lookah! A garland in honah of a Garland!" She got up and put it all around the tree, surrounding the cross-stitched R and the wheelbarrow with Barrett.

"Mom," I said, "popcorn garlands shouldn't be kept after Christmas is over. Neither should this tradition. I'm going to be an unmarried twenty-six-year-old with a Christmas tree full of ornaments of boys I used to know!!" She gasped at the word "unmarried."

"Don't say that Clovah!" Under her breath she muttered five times, "You WILL get married Clovah Mannahhouse." As though saying it over and over would make something right that was terribly wrong.

After remembering these very special things about my mom, I refocused on my dad, who was still trying to convince us how normal we were. I interrupted him.

"Dad … Dad! … DAD!!!" I had to get his attention. "I don't want to move. Wherever we go … there we are. Mom can be invisible here. She blends in. Los Angeles is big. You know what I mean?"

My dad looked at me sort of defeated, but also with understanding. I tried to help him see more clearly, "Did I tell you that when Mom was putting groceries in the car at the store the other day, she left three doors open while she returned the cart? The car next to us was honking and yelling because they were ready to leave, but they couldn't pull out with all those doors open. Mom yelled back at them, 'Hold yah horses! I can't walk that fast with these awesome heels mistah!'" I used my best Maggie Ann Mannerhouse expression. Dad smiled. He was obviously not on my side.

Dad loved Mom's little quirks. He adored them actually. He would always grab her in the kitchen and say in his lawyer ad voice, "I'll represent YOU!" I didn't get it, but if he wanted to "represent" her, I certainly didn't care.

After telling my dad the grocery cart story, my mom came out from behind the kitchen and said, "I'm right here, Clovah!" and to that I replied, "Mom, nothing about you is a secret. Of course you are right here … you are everywhere. You are tiny, but you fill the whole house." It wasn't a compliment, but she smiled like it was and said, "Aw, thank you sweetie." She sat down with all of us at the table and did something that actually caused me to raise the white flag in surrender to moving.

She said, "Everyone's pointah fingah in the middle with mine. Come on. We're going to make this move …" and we all said in unison, "Toogethah!"

The Move-In

The second I stepped foot on Hitlery soil my mom announced, "I know you are worried about moving Clovah, so I signed you up for a club. It's called Alpha Omega. Your first meeting is this Thursday." She immediately ran off to help my dad unload the trunk of our very full station wagon in her "work shoes," shoes that had a platform heel, rather than the usual spike heel.

I didn't say a word. I couldn't. The whole family was in task mode and was moving stuff from the station wagon to the house. My mom may come off as a naïve ditz, but she is actually pretty smart. Shrewd is a better word for it. She dropped the "You are joining a club" bomb right when the bustle of activity exploded so that there was no way I could say anything. I did what any other immature thirteen-year-old would do at a time like that. I protested by not helping unpack and muttered rebellious remarks under my breath. "I'll sign you up for a club … the only club worth trying is a Club sandwich …"

My brother was walking back to the car for another load, and I muttered, "I'd like to give you a knuckle sandwich." He didn't hear me but noticed I was standing there sulking and doing nothing. He gave me an ugly face, and I said, "You look better that way." I took my anger out on my brother. I wasn't worried about moving before, but now I was. I hated it when my mom forced me to do things without asking first. I wasn't three anymore.

"Someone needs some Bad Attitude medicine!" she said as she came out for her second load. "Tom, your daughter needs some B.A. medicine. Good thing your dad is wearing his comfy sweats, Clovah."

"I'm sorry Mom, no, I'll help. PLEASE don't. Not here. I'll join any club you want. We JUST moved here. Don't. I didn't think you would ever do that again, Dad! I'll help."

It was too late. My dad was standing on the side of the road waiting for a car to come by with his back turned to the road. B.A. medicine was the worst. Los Angeles was a big, rude city with lots of crass people, especially in our neighborhood. So when I was eight and I talked back to my dad for the first time in a major way, he went outside and mooned the first car that drove by. He came back inside and looked me in the eyes and said, "That there is B.A. medicine. B.A. stands for Bad Attitude, and also Bare … Butt." (Remember my parents don't swear?) "Some medicines taste worse than others," he said. I died inside a little bit that day and NEVER talked back to either of my parents again.

After my mom announced I needed that same medicine again on the first day we moved to Hitlery, I grabbed a suitcase from the back of the station wagon to show that I had really and truly changed my attitude. I ran in the house before a car could drive by. I sat on the suitcase, waited by the front window, and watched as my dad was about to use up our first impression ticket. We only had one. My heart was beating out of my chest. What was he DOING!?!?!

I heard a car coming. I looked up to see my dad, hands on his waistband, ready to rob us of our dignity. I could see the driver clearly. She was about twenty years older than my mom with very natural uncolored short hair that was half grey. Her car window was rolled down.

I looked at my dad. He crossed his arms over his chest, making the love sign, then pointed to me. He didn't do it … he didn't do it! I broke out in a cold sweat. I ran out and literally cried in his arms, "Thank you, thank you, Dad! I will join Mom's stupid club. I won't sulk anymore."

He wrapped his arms around me and said, "Ah Clover, I wasn't gonna do it. I just meant to scare you a little bit to let you know I was still your dad, even in a new town."

I stopped crying and said, "How about next time you fold my dinner napkin into a rabbit like you do sometimes. That's a better dad trick." I could tell by the feel of his chest muscles that he was smiling.

I went back in the house to take a look at all the rooms. The house was still pretty empty because the moving van had not yet arrived. This house was way bigger than our little apartment in Los Angeles, and I explored on my own before my mom and dad gave us the parental tour. It occurred to me that I had the opportunity to do something I had never gotten to do—look in my mom and dad's bedroom.

In Los Angeles, their bedroom was always locked. They said it was because of cleaning purposes. They had a tiny bathroom connected to their room, and they didn't want us to be tempted to go in and use it. Dad insisted that we stay out because he didn't want my mom to have to clean two bathrooms that were used by the kids. When I was little I accepted that, but the older I got, I felt like I was missing something by being banished from their bedroom, but I didn't know what. It was like that door represented something. I wanted in. Or, I didn't want to be shut out. Something.

Standing in the hall, I knew that one of these bedrooms would belong to my parents, and that I could see it before it was declared off limits. I walked into the biggest bedroom, and there was a bathroom inside along with a huge closet. It was spacious and beautiful. For a minute I thought I should try to beg for that room, but then the vision of my dad standing on the side of the street giving me B.A. medicine made me think otherwise. I would take the smallest room and be quiet. I went into the bathroom and marveled at the huge tub with jets. I was feeling the smooth countertops and noticing my blemishes in the mirror when my mom walked in. She got stiff as a board.

She did something I had never seen her do. She freaked out and started screaming, "Get out, Clovah … get OUT!!!!" Her eyes started blinking fast like they did before she normally left the room to cry, but there was nowhere for her to go. I was right in the place she usually ran to. She was standing in front of the door, so I couldn't leave. I eventually felt brave enough to squeeze by her manic self and get out.

"Okay, Mom. I'm sorry. I didn't know. The room was empty, so I thought it would be okay. I didn't even use the toilet or make it dirty, I promise! I'm leaving."

Right then, I knew that there must be more to the locked bedroom than just keeping it clean. She slammed the bathroom door behind me and started running the bath water.

Between the B.A. stunt my dad pulled and my mom freaking out, I had had enough drama for the day. I took the opportunity to have a moment alone. My dad and Ryan were busy checking out the back yard. My mom had locked herself in the bathroom to drown her mysterious sorrows with hot water. I really hoped it would work.

I arranged our things into the common space, and my dad came in and gave my brother and me a tour. Before I could say anything, my brother chose his room first, like a dog peeing on his territory. Brothers are so annoying.

Soon after that, the moving guys came with the rest of our furniture and boxed stuff. My dad gave my brother the keys to the station wagon and told him to use his smart phone to find something for us to do for a couple hours. It was nice that he could drive. At least he was good for something.

We decided to check out the famous Millie Hitlery Hotel. We sat in the hotel restaurant, drank milkshakes, and read the legacy of Hitlery printed on the back of the menu:

> *Manning Hitlery messed up a lot of marriages. Not because he inappropriately loved other wives, but because he lavishly loved his. Back in the 1930s when housewives were stuck at home, lonely and forgotten, Manning adored and lifted up his wife, Millie. He did everything different than the world around him. He let his wife be an equal partner in the marriage. He let her drive. He brought her to town meetings and let her speak for the both of them. He introduced her to the builders, and she helped him make decisions about the family mansion they built that overlooked the city. People even say that their bank account was in both their names. As the story goes, the teller wasn't going to allow it, but when Manning plunked down a briefcase with $300,000 in cash, the branch manager didn't care whose names were on the account. After the couple died, their house was given to their one and only daughter. She turned it into a hotel and held a national essay contest. For the grand prize, she would give the house away to a worthy couple. The only thing the daughter insisted on was that the hotel be named after her mother, Millie Hitlery, because that's what her father would have wanted. Soon after, the city was also named after the fortunate couple with the unfortunate name.*

When my brother and I went back home, the movers were setting up the beds in our rooms, and my mom was looking through boxes, trying to find the linens. I sat on the couch and watched her. I always thought she was pretty, but in a white bread sort of way. I wondered if Millie Hitlery was at all like my mother. I wondered about her daughter and if she was allowed to go in her parent's bedroom. I wondered if Manning Hitlery would've treated Millie the same if she had been crazy like my mother. Maybe she was. Maybe Manning was just an amazing man who always treated his wife like a queen, no matter what. I could understand why the menu said that Manning had messed up a lot of marriages. I was ready to leave and go live at the hotel. I bet there weren't any locked doors there.

Down the hall, I could see that my parent's bedroom door was shut again. The hallway looked empty. I thought about being inside my mom's room that morning. I was disappointed to think that those two minutes in their bedroom suite was all I would get.

Probably ever.

The Fundraiser

A couple days later, that very Thursday, I went to the club my mom had registered me for, Alpha Omega. It was a Christian club, and I wondered if she knew that when she signed me up.

Alpha Omega was an odd thing. It was like going to a sports game where a bunch of girls celebrated a team they couldn't see. I sat with them but felt like an outsider, like a person wearing the opposing team's color.

They sang songs and a couple girls even reached their hands up like they were expecting high fives from God. I was embarrassed for them. It was my first time being around Christians who sang together. There was no way I was going to sing. I sat there and pretended I had something in my eye. Singing with people is not normal. The only time I had ever sung along with a crowd was when a friend took me to a rock concert and we screamed like schoolgirls. But that wasn't technically singing.

Both the girls and the leaders at Alpha Omega were nice enough. After my mom signed me up online, the leaders contacted her, so she knew where to take me. We drove into the

Hitlery Church parking lot. "Are you sure this isn't a Communist Club, Mom?" I asked when I saw the sign. "Naw, Clovah, it's just an unfortunate name for a town." I thought that was funny because that's exactly how the menu had described the name of Hitlery: unfortunate.

"The leader sounded real nice on the phone. You should meet some good kids here," she said. Apparently my mom was willing to risk me converting to a cheesy faith as long as I got in with the right crowd. Desperation leads us to do many things in life that are down a different alley.

When we walked in the lobby, I was smacked with the reality of what it was going to be like to live with non-Los Angeles people. We were different.

My mom had on her long, straight blond wig. I was grateful for that because it was her least fake looking one. Her dress was really flowing and wispy, and she wore so much makeup that you could paint a picture if you wiped your finger on her face and rubbed it on a piece of paper. Her shoes were bright red and spiky. She walked well in them. If we ever needed to come up with $40,000 real quick, like in the movies, I would enter my mom in a high heel-walking contest, and she would save the day with her commitment to buying ridiculous shoes.

All the other kids and their moms were wearing plain Jane clothes that were modest and natural. Regular sandals and regular hair and regular clothes. The women leaders had nice hair that was all their own. There were no fake wigs that I could see. One girl had a very impressive hat, and it looked like she was covering up a bald head underneath. I thought that she and my mom might cancel each other out if they stood next to each other.

After I signed the attendance sheet and was welcomed by the leaders, my mom left and I was all alone with fifty other middle school girls. I was paired up with another girl named Twinkle, who was also new. Before I could ask her about her name she said, "My parents are hippies from Colorado. I was born in a birthing pool outside in our backyard. It was night. A very starry night. Thus … Twinkle." She looked bored by it. "As soon as I'm eighteen, I'm changing my name to Sally. It's common and wonderful!"

"My family is weird too," I said.

The meeting started, and they asked us to stand up if we were new, so Twinkle and I did. Twinkle actually exaggerated a curtsy and waved to everyone. I just stared straight ahead and sat down real quick. I was nervous because I wasn't sure what they did at these Christian events. My only friend in Los Angeles who went to church said that in her youth group, they had them go up front and do things that were silly and fun. I didn't see anything that looked like we would have to be put on the spot. No silly skit props where they would be looking for volunteers, so that was good news. I was not going to volunteer for anything, that's for sure. There was no way I was doing that.

When the singing was over, a woman got up to talk to us. She was a real nice lady, and she didn't seem TOO pushy. I can't remember a word she said because I was zoning out, just trying to survive.

At the end of her talk, Twinkle seemed excited. "What?" I asked.

"Weren't you listening?" Twinkle muttered. "We are all going to Disneyland together at the end of the year. She's passing out the catalogs now for the fundraiser we are doing for the trip." I had always wanted to go to Disneyland, but my parents could never shake it financially.

When the catalog came to me, I was indifferent. It was fifty pages long, full of trinkets and gadgets that family and friends supposedly could not live without. Knowing that our family always had trouble making ends meet and knowing that our tribe was small, I knew I probably wouldn't raise enough money to go. At the very least, I would be able to contribute to the family magazine pile.

My dad was selling things all day now, so I thought he might be able to take it to work. Maybe sellers buy.

The Challenge

"You are going, Clovah, I don't care if we have to go door to door!" That's what my mom said when she picked me up from the meeting and saw my fundraising catalog.

"Maybe Dad will take the catalog to work and sell stuff for me there. You never know," I said, hoping I wouldn't have to go knocking on doors. My mom was set on me taking this trip, but I couldn't imagine walking up to houses and selling to people I didn't know. How humiliating.

When we got home, my dad was just arriving from his long day of staring at a camera to convince people to buy stuff they didn't need. My mom showed him my catalog, and he rolled his eyes and groaned. "UGH, I can't look at another product after a day of selling things!"

"Of course!" I whispered under my breath. "Door to door it is." I went in my room to feel sorry for myself.

My room wasn't fancy, but it had one feature I really loved— my brother wasn't in it. Since we never had any extra money, I had never been able to decorate my room with anything special.

But when we moved to Hitlery, my mom thought she would cel-ebrate the new wiggle room in our budget by going to Target to get me decorations. Just my luck, there was a back-to-college clearance section, and she came home with bags full of gaudy fuzzy pillows, lamps, and blankets. Now my room looked like a troll doll had felt sorry for me and donated its hair to my cause. Instead of Locks of Love, it's Locks of Troll Love. I thought about telling her that we could've saved money and made decora-tions out of her wigs if we were going for the hair look. I decided against that.

Instead of crying myself to sleep about selling things door to door, I sucked it up and went to my closet to pick out the out-fit I would wear. Something normal that grown-ups would find respectable.

As I looked for an outfit, I imagined the conversation I would have when people answered their door. It went something like this:

"Hello young lady!"

"Hello, my name is Clover, and I'm selling stuff to raise money for a trip to Disneyland. I wondered if you would be interested in helping me?"

"Disneyland, eh? Well that sounds fun. What group are you going with?"

"Alpha Omega."

"A Christian group is going to Disneyland? What for anyway? Are you going to try to save Mickey Mouse? I hear he's a bad, bad mouse!"

"Yeah, I don't know why we are going actually. To have fun I guess?"

"Hmmmm. Well if you don't know why you are going, then I don't know why I should buy anything."

"Okay. Thank you anyway."

I just couldn't picture anyone buying something from a girl whose mom signed her up for a club that she didn't want to go to, for a trip that didn't make sense. I guess Maggie Ann Manner-house needed to see for herself that it was useless.

All the awkwardness of Alpha Omega and thoughts about the fundraiser distracted me from an even greater event that was headed my way the very next day. The first day of school.

The next morning we got in the car, and my mom went on and on about how perfect it was that I had gone to Alpha Omega and met some kids, so I could have some friends on my first day. Then if it went real rotten, I could have the weekend to recuperate.

I wondered why she was so worried about me and why she was trying to manage my life. I snapped. "Why don't you come on in and make my friends for me, Mom? You could even make an ornament to represent them for Christmas!!" I could tell that I hurt her feelings because she started blinking real fast. I got out of the car and said, "Make your own friends, Mom, for the first time ever!!!" She drove away quickly.

The middle school was small. Kids walked in the front door like they were going into their own home, comfortable and famil-iar. I felt like you do when you try a new food. I was convinced that I would hate it. Everyone was staring at me. I remembered how at my old school, a new kid was either everyone's new friend or they were old news by the end of the first day. I was just hoping for kindness.

"Hey new girl!" It was Twinkle. She was in the office, too, and I was so glad to see her. "Hey," I said back, trying to be real chill with my voice. I wasn't scared to death, but I admit that I was nervous. The secretary gave me my schedule, and immedi-ately Twinkle and I looked to see if we had any classes together. One of the students took us to our lockers and gave us a tour. The building was easy to get around since it was such a small school. Nothing like the middle schools in Los Angeles, where you had to go in and out of buildings to get to a class and even walk out-side sometimes. This was just one building. I looked at Twinkle and said, "This seems a little too easy. I hope there is something challenging in this little town of Hitlery. I haven't seen anyone fighting in the halls, and I'm pretty sure I'll be able to find all my classes."

Right then a girl came out of the bathroom and saw Twinkle. With bright mocking eyes she looked at her and said, "I've heard about you, new kid! You are Twinkle, Twinkle Little Star!!!"

I was surprised at Twinkle's response. She looked at her watch and said, "Wow … ten minutes. I thought for SURE that would happen sooner." Then she put her hand out to shake and said, "How I wonder what YOU are? Because I know what I am."

The girl walked away without winning the prize she thought she might collect by teasing someone new. I looked at Twinkle with awe and said, "That isn't the first time that has happened to you I'm guessing?"

"You have NO idea," Twinkle said.

At lunch I found Twinkle pretty easily, and she had already found some Alpha Omega girls to sit with. Maybe my mom was right, but I would never tell her. It was nice to see familiar faces. The girls joked about all the stuff they did last summer, and Twinkle and I sat there bored. I whispered to Twinkle, "Hey do you want to come over after school? I'll text my mom to see if it's okay."

She answered back, "Sure, just don't let the teachers see you texting, or they will take your phone away."

"Oh yeah, small school." No one in Los Angeles cared if I had a cell phone in school, except in class of course, but outside of class, it was a texting frenzy.

My mom picked us up after school, and I could tell she was thrilled that I was already having a friend over. Twinkle and I tried to get past that awkward new friend stage by going through the music we liked. We checked out the music on my phone, and she showed me some stuff that I might like on hers.

"Have you ever listened to any Christian music?" she asked.

"No way!" I said, but then I wondered if I should've been so honest. Did she like that stuff?

"I know you didn't know any of the songs that we sang last night at Alpha Omega," she said, "so I thought I would show you a radio station that you can listen to. You know, in case you want the songs to be more familiar to you." She led me to the station's website. It was full of things to read, scripture, and chat rooms for different topics. It was totally boring, so I changed the subject.

"Are you going to sell stuff for that trip?" I asked Twinkle.

"I don't know. My parents will probably just pay for it," she said.

"Lucky!!" I said as I laid back on my bed in protest.

"Why? Do you have to sell stuff to go?" she asked.

"Not ONLY do I have to sell it. My dad won't take it to work, so I have to go door to door." I looked at her for much needed sympathy.

"BUMMER!" she said and we sat in silence for a while. "Hey why don't we take a walk and scout out the best houses that we think will be the easiest. You don't want to do that with your mom, right? Maybe we can do the first house together?" When I heard her say together, I repeated it in my brain and pictured my mom's fingers joining, "toogethah!" and I couldn't resist her invitation.

The neighborhood was so different from what I was used to. There were houses with yards and people out and about who said hello. One house that looked really cute had a wreath on the front door. The yard was well kept, and there were a couple of really nice cars parked out front.

"I bet they have money," I said. "Strictly from a selling stand-point of course."

"You should go right now, Clover. Do it before you have to go with your mom tomorrow," Twinkle said. She pulled my catalog out from under her shirt and gave it to me.

"I didn't know you brought that with us, Twinkle!" I stared at her. "You do it!"

"No … YOU do it!" she said. She stood on the sidewalk and was clearly not budging. "I'll wait right here for you."

I walked up to the porch and rang the doorbell. When the door opened, I froze. Standing in front of me was the same woman who drove by in the car when my father was ready to give me the B.A. medicine. My face turned red and I wanted to run away. "I'm sorry … I mean … I am Clover, and I am selling something … it's for Disneyland." I had to concentrate so my words would make a sentence.

She put her hand on my shoulder and said, "Clover, welcome. I am one of the leaders at Alpha Omega, and I'd love to buy something from you. Come in." She motioned for Twinkle to come in too.

"I am Mrs. Belle and I, blah blah blah …" is all I heard. I was too busy being horrified that I was in the house of the woman my dad almost mooned, and she was a LEADER at Alpha Omega. Thank God he didn't do it, but she must have seen him standing there with his hands on his pants? What did she think about me and my family?

"I was expecting you. I told your mom to bring you by tomorrow morning, but I'm glad you came on your own. I have an envelope for you. I'd like you to go on the trip to Disneyland, so here's my donation with my order. Please go look at it and keep it in a safe place. I'll be seeing you Thursday nights alright?" She gave me the envelope and I said, "Thank you, Mrs. Belle."

We calmly walked out of her house, but as soon as we were out of sight, I booked it all the way home. I heard Twinkle from behind, trying to catch up with me, "Clover, wait up! What's the big hurry? Clooooovvvveeerrrr!!!!"

We got home and I pulled Twinkle in my room and shut the door. I told her all about the B.A. medicine and Mrs. Belle. She could easily sympathize with me. We ughed about my dad for a while, and she told me her dad horror stories.

When Twinkle was five, she and a friend found some pull-up diapers in the basement storage. They put them on over their pants and wore them around the house to play babies. She had forgotten about it until last year when some people at church started teasing her about it. Her dad had posted the picture on his social media site for Throwback Thursday, the day of the week when parents post embarrassing pictures of themselves or their kids when they were younger—without their permission. Twinkle said it wouldn't have been so bad except that she was standing right by her crush when she first got teased about it.

I figured it was time to look at Mrs. Belle's order to see what I needed to sell the next day and opened the envelope. Inside was a check for $1,000. There was a note that I read to Twinkle. It said:

The Challenge:

Use this money to buy $1,000 worth of products. Here are the rules.

1. *Nothing can be used for yourself.*
2. *Give everything in secret.*
3. *Be a light.*
4. *Love your enemies.*
5. *Find treasure.*
6. *Ask and it will be given you.*
7. *Build your house on rock.*
8. *Use what you have to be welcomed.*
9. *Go to Disneyland and have fun!!!*

Twinkle was smiling. I didn't think this was funny at all. "What is this!? I don't understand it!" I said very honestly.

Twinkle looked at me very smugly and said, "It's a challenge. I seem to remember that just this morning you said you were looking for a challenge in this little town. Am I wrong?"

No. I didn't believe she was wrong. Gosh DARN IT!!

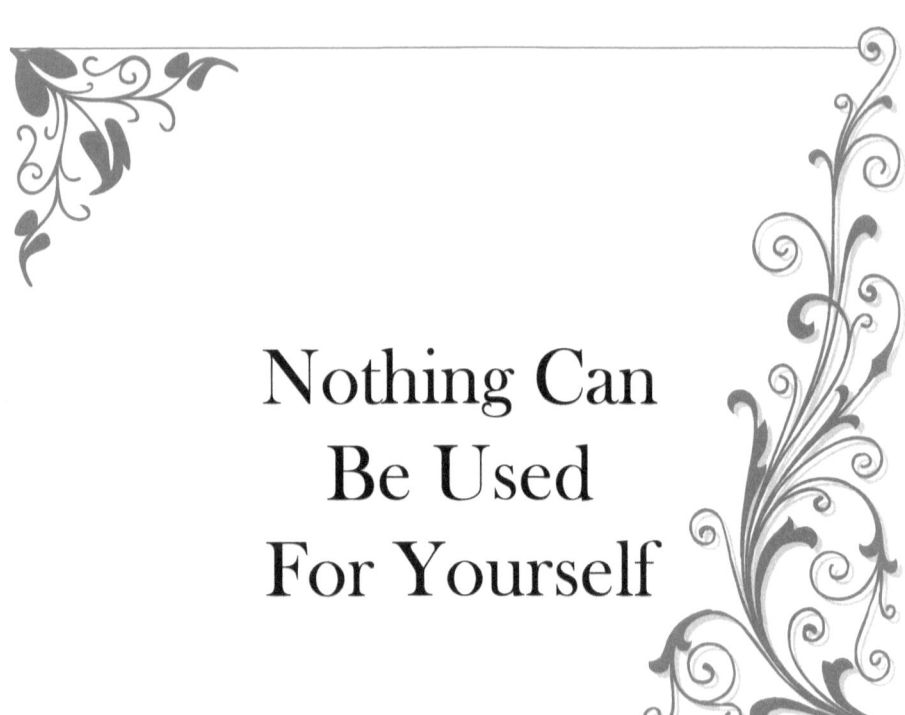

Nothing Can
Be Used
For Yourself

*T*hat night I looked at the note again and was grateful for rule number one: *Nothing can be used for yourself.* That was clear. I couldn't buy anything for myself. Check. I could do that.

At least that's what I thought—until I opened the catalog and started looking through all the cool stuff inside.

They had everything from key chains to two person bicycles to huge stuff like RV rentals. You could rent an RV from a national company, but they were only stationed out of certain cities, so you either had to live nearby or be able to get there. That made it a little limited, but how cool was that?

So many things were going through my head as I looked through the catalog and thought about the rules of The Challenge. If I did it wrong would I be told I couldn't go to Disneyland? Who would ever know if I broke the first rule and bought something for myself? What if I just spent the money on gifts for my family? Would that still fulfill all the rules? I had only three weeks to crack the code, fill out my order, and turn it in for the fundraiser. Who would explain rule #6, *Ask and it will be given you*? Who would tell me what #3, *Be a light,* meant? Did Mrs. Belle expect me to go back to her house and ask her? I did not want go back there, and now that I knew she went to Alpha Omega, I wanted to be sure to avoid her.

When I woke up the next morning, I heard my parents talking in the kitchen.

"Do you really think Clover will sell enough of that stuff to get to Disneyland, Maggie?" my dad asked.

"I don't know, Tom, but I want her to try," my mom replied.

"But what happens if she tries and doesn't make it?" he asked. "We can't afford to send her. Disneyland costs over $100 a day, plus there's the cost of food, the bus fee, and everything else. What's going to happen if she makes all these friends at Alpha Omega, and she's the only one who can't go?"

"She'll do what we all do when we are disappointed … she'll go buy shoes!" she said. Then I think my mom threw a pancake at my dad because he said, "Hey! Gross, Maggie. We don't have a dog to eat that you know." I figured it was time to put them out of their misery about the situation.

"You don't have to worry about me raising money to go on the trip," I said.

"Clovah, you are GOING, and that's final. Tom! I knew she would hear us talking and would worry. You are going to raise enough money, don't even worry." My mom pointed her fork at my dad and mouthed something accusing like it was all his fault.

"I'm not worried," I said. "A surprise happened yesterday."

"A surprise?" they said together, and then they started talking over each other, "What kind of surprise?" and "We never get surprises."

"You remember Mrs. Belle? I think that's her name. You know, that leader that talked to you about Alpha Omega? She said she asked you to bring me over to her house today, so I could sell to her," I said.

"Is she the one who owns the shopping channel I work for?" my dad asked. "The Belles? I knew he lived somewhere in this neighborhood. Heaven knows why he lives in a regular neighborhood like this. He could be anywhere. That man has millions, I'm sure."

I chimed in real quickly, "Yeah, and she's the one you almost MOONED when you were going to give me the B.A. Medicine!" I hoped that would teach him a lesson.

"Yeah, yeah," my mom said. "She told me about the Alpha Omega Club when Dad got the job, and she helped me get acquainted with the area. Go on, go on ..." My mom rolled her hands real fast, trying to make me spit the words out faster.

I decided not to share the whole note with them, especially not The Challenge part, "Well she sort of bought $1,000 worth of stuff, so I could go on the trip."

They stared at me.

"Say something," I said.

"One thousand dollars as in A THOUSAND DOLLARS, Clover?" my dad asked.

"Yes," I said, which made more sense now that I knew that the Belles owned the shopping network where my dad worked. They had money and wanted to help an employee out. Sort of like buying a ton of Girl Scout cookies or something.

They looked at me a little longer and said, "Dang."

I could tell that their world was rocked. I could tell that nothing like this had ever happened to them before. They were going to need some time to think, so I thought I would remove myself. "I'm going to my room now, since we don't need to go door to door after all. Is that okay, Mom?"

She didn't say anything, so I went up to her, "Okay, Mom?"

She seemed to snap out of it, "Yeah, okay, Clovah." She started blinking real fast, got up, went to her bedroom, and locked the door like she does when she is running away from something. This time I didn't know what was so terrible. I could hear the bath water running. I looked at my dad. "Does she do that so we won't hear her crying?"

He did a quick breathe out. "You're a smart girl, Clover. Let's just say you never heard it from me, alright?"

"Alright. I'll be in my room looking through the catalog of all the things I can't buy," I lied.

"Sounds like what I do every day at my job. It's no fun, but knock yourself out," he said. I had never thought about his job like that before—that he had to handle beautiful items like diamonds and purses and blenders that he would never be able to buy for my mom or himself.

That gave me an idea.

It took a whole day to look through the catalog. Several hours and twelve rough drafts later, I finally had my final order. The hardest part was trying to get all the things I wanted for under $1,000. I didn't know how all the stuff would be used, but I knew who they would be for. A beautiful diamond ring, five thousand glow sticks, a blender, a toaster oven, a baby pool, two crystal goblets, and an RV rented for one night. I sort of cheated on that last one because I bought a little something for myself. I was going to use the RV for an end-of-year eighth grade graduation sleepover.

At that point, I didn't care about the rules anymore. I just wanted to turn in the order, so I could stop thinking about it. I folded up the form and placed it in the envelope with the $1,000 check from Mrs. Belle. I called Twinkle and said, "What's your address? I need to hide $1,000 worth of stuff at your house."

The Speaker

That next week at Alpha Omega, I was excited to turn in my order. My mom came in with me so she could thank Mrs. Belle. We still had two weeks left to sell the products, so I wasn't sure there would even be a place to turn in the order form yet.

When we walked into the foyer, a couple girls were sitting at a table under a sign that read, "Disneyland Fundraiser." The girl on the left was the one I'd seen at the first meeting with the cool hat, hiding what I thought was a bald head. Only this time she wasn't wearing a hat. She was just sitting there with her sweet, naked, smooth round head. As soon as my mom saw her, she stopped dead in her tracks, turned around, and got all blinky. She left without even saying goodbye. I looked at the girls and shrugged.

"Sometimes moms have their own agenda," I said, and they laughed nervously.

"I'm used to it," the bald girl said with confidence. "My name is Lisa. My small group leader and I are going through a Bible study together for cancer patients and survivors. It's really good.

The study encourages us to go bald, so that's what I do when I'm out in public where people know me and I feel safe. I don't go bald at school, but I know I am loved and accepted here. Does your mom have cancer?"

"Excuse me?" I asked, caught totally off guard.

She must have seen a look of horror on my face because she recoiled and was so embarrassed, "I'm sorry. Sometimes I get so used to talking about my life that I forget that a thing like cancer is really private. I just noticed that she wears a wig, that's all. It's none of my business. Please, forgive me!"

"I just … I was surprised that's all. We used to live in Los Angeles. That's why she wears a wig. It's what people did out there," I said.

I regained some composure, but in my heart I was still startled. It's like someone saying, "Why is your house black? Was it on fire at one point?" No one else has a black house, but you are so used to living in it that you firmly believe everyone has a black house. You would never question the reason—it's just a black house. I felt like my eyes had been shut and now they were opened to the question I had never asked before. Why DID my mom wear a wig? Even if that's what people did in Los Angeles, why didn't she take it off now?

I stood there in a daze, and Lisa saw my order form. "No way! You got the $1,000 order from Mrs. Belle, didn't you?" and she took it from me.

"Yes. How did you know?" I asked eagerly. There was obviously a story there.

"Every year Mrs. Belle buys $1,000 worth of stuff from someone … well … sort of." She looked at me like I knew what she meant by that.

"You mean, she doesn't actually buy the stuff," I started to say, but then she interrupted me.

"EXACTLY!" She pointed her finger at me like I had won the lottery.

"I don't think it's so exciting," I said. "I'd like to talk to the person who got it last year, so I can get some hints about whether or not I bought the right kind of stuff. It's all a mysterious code, and I hope I cracked it."

"You're looking at her," Lisa said. "It changed my life. You are in for it girl, and that's all I'm going to say!" She put her fingers over her lips, zipped them up, and threw away the key.

"What? You mean the same thing happened to you last year? What did you buy? How did you solve the riddles? What if I did it wrong?"

I asked so many questions that she got up and put her arm around me. "I know," she said. "Relax. Why don't you go find a seat and listen to the speaker? I think that will answer a lot of your questions."

I looked in the room where all the kids were congregating, and Lisa motioned with her eyes for me to go in. She put her fingers over her lips to zip them again and walked back to the table to help the other girls who had brought in their forms.

I caught Twinkle's eye, and she patted the seat next to her that she had saved for me. I recognized a girl who was sitting way in the back, all alone. She was the girl who stood at the bus stop with me every morning. She was beautiful, intimidatingly beautiful. I had said hello to her every morning and she was nice enough, but it was clear to me that she wasn't interested in being friends. I figured someone that pretty was probably so popular that she didn't need another friend. But seeing her be so lonely at Alpha Omega made me wonder about her. It also made me glad I had met Twinkle on the first night. That could be me sitting there by myself.

After enduring a couple songs that I didn't know, the speaker came out and, lo and behold, it was Mrs. Belle. So much for avoiding her. She explained that we would discuss a different topic each month, and then she looked right at me when she said our first topic would be *"Nothing can be used for yourself!"* It was rule #1 of The Challenge. She gave me a look like she had winked, but she hadn't. Her brain winked. I nodded slowly in her direction as if to say, *I get it. I see your connection to the challenge you gave me, Mrs. Belle.* Clever. So that's the big plan.

When she looked away, I shook my head in disappointment. She had tricked me. She gave me something I really wanted, a trip to Disneyland, and my ticket to go was The Challenge, which had rules that could only be learned by coming to Alpha Omega. I didn't want to play her little game. I wanted to get my coat, take back my order form, and leave. I could always call my mom and ask her to come get me out of this little rat trap she had signed me up for, but then Mrs. Belle started in with her speech.

"Ladies, I am so glad you are here." Immediately winsome with just one phrase. Not just winsome, but motherly—and genuine. I believed she was glad I was there. That felt good. I felt wanted. It would've been so much easier just to walk out if her words didn't feel like homemade cookies to my soul.

"We are basing our series this year on Matthew 5 and 6, the Sermon on the Mount. We will be jumping around a bit, and tonight we are going to start off with our theme for the whole year: Treasure.

"Listen to Matthew 6:19-21. It says, *'Do not lay up for yourselves treasures on earth, where moth and rust destroy and where thieves break in and steal, but lay up for yourselves treasures in heaven, where neither moth nor rust destroys and where thieves do not break in and steal. For where your treasure is, there your heart will be also.'"*

Mrs. Belle finished reading and motioned for the ninth grade helpers to wheel in a huge treasure box. While they were pushing it to her she said, "This box is full of something that all middle school girls want!"

A couple girls couldn't contain themselves, "What? What's in there?"

"Earthly treasure," Mrs. Belle said. "The scripture says there are two kinds of treasure. Earthly treasure and heavenly treasure. This big box has earthly treasure. Do you want to see what's inside?"

We all wanted to see. The box was beautiful. Not ornately beautiful but rustic and sturdy.

"If you want to have what's inside, then come up here." She waited to give time for the girls to make their way up front. Some girls rushed, especially the girls that were close. Twinkle got up to go up front, but I stayed behind.

"Come on Clover!" Twinkle said. "Don't you want the treasure?"

"No that's okay. I'll watch," I lied. I did want it but felt too out of place to be up front. I noticed that some other girls stayed in their seats, and I was glad I wasn't the only one who just felt like watching.

Mrs. Belle took a bag from behind the treasure box that was full of long rags and said, "We are going to play a game. You will all be blindfolded. Once you have the blindfold secured over your eyes, you will have two choices. You can either have earthly treasure from the treasure box, or you can have heavenly treasure.

"If you go for earthly treasure, it might be stolen from you. BUT it's really awesome. If you go for heavenly treasure, it won't be taken away, but you have to trust that it will be good. You can think about which one to choose while we put the blindfolds on."

The ninth grade helpers passed out the blindfolds and helped put them on. Once they had everyone taken care of, Mrs. Belle announced, "Raise your hand if you want earthly treasure. It will be amazing, but remember there is a chance that you won't be able to keep it. It could be stolen from you."

Half the girls raised their hands, and I watched as Mrs. Belle and the ninth grade helpers gave each of them a brand new iPhone. All the girls gasped when they held their new phone, and one girl even said, "Is this an iPhone, Mrs. Belle?" The girls who didn't choose earthly treasure could hear how happy the other girls were and moaned in disappointment. "NO FAIR!!" they shouted. Someone even said, "Can we change our mind?"

"Yes!" Mrs. Belle said. "Now that you know what you are missing, you can change your mind, but remember, if you choose the earthly treasure, it might be stolen." Several girls raised their hands and got an iPhone instead of heavenly treasure like they first chose.

The girls who stuck with heavenly treasure could now take off their blindfolds and sit in a group and watch. Mrs. Belle gave them fuzzy, silky throw blankets that were warm and super soft. The girls with the iPhones still wore the blindfolds and couldn't see the cozy friendship huddle of the blanket girls.

"I want the girls who are still wearing blindfolds to walk around and try to find each other. When you find someone, tap them on the shoulder. If you tap them first, they have to give you their phone." Some of the girls groaned in disappointment. They could see now that the odds were against them to keep their phones. Everyone became competitive. Girls stood with their arms outstretched to keep others away, even though the exercise had not started.

"Are you ready?" Mrs. Belle asked. Clearly they were not, but that didn't stop her from saying, "GO!" I watched as the group of girls frantically tried not to get their phones taken. Some girls walked around flapping their arms, so they could say that they tapped first. It got nasty. Some girls argued over who tapped who first. Others pouted when their phones were taken away.

What Mrs. Belle didn't reveal was that *she* could also tap the girls and take their phones. Without wearing a blindfold, she casually walked around and tapped every girl, took her phone, and put it back in the treasure box—until no one had a phone anymore.

The blindfolds came off, and they all looked around to see who still had a phone. They were shocked. "No one got to keep it Mrs. Belle? Not one?" I could tell they had expected some of the girls to have at least two or three phones. "Where did they go?" they wanted to know.

Mrs. Belle pointed to the treasure box. "In here," she said. "Go ahead and go back to your seats." She pointed to the group of heavenly treasure girls. "You girls can stay right there."

At that point, the earthly treasure group saw that there were eight girls huddled together with cozy, soft throw blankets that they got to keep, and they were immediately jealous. Twinkle was right there among them, wrapped in her heavenly treasure. "Aw man!" the other girls said. "How come THEY get to keep their blankets?"

One no-phone girl piped up and said, "She warned us, but we didn't listen. We all had a chance for the sure thing, and we didn't take it." Mrs. Belle nodded in agreement.

"That's right," she said. "You all knew that if you went for earthly treasure, there was a chance that it would be taken. I do admit that I tricked you. I didn't tell you that losing the item was guaranteed, but that's because I wanted you to struggle with the choice."

She looked at the group of girls with the blankets. "It's easy to know what earthly treasure is—phones, clothes, houses, cars, and the stuff of life. But we don't talk about heavenly treasure much," she said. "In fact, most of us have heard the saying that when we die, 'You can't take it with you.' So if we can't take anything with us to heaven, then what is heavenly treasure?"

One girl shouted, "Cozy blankets?" The girls laughed. I didn't. I was not sure how to process what I was seeing and hearing.

Another girl said, "God?" I could tell that Mrs. Belle appreciated the interaction. She seemed to genuinely enjoy the group.

She answered her own question with a ridiculous claim. "It's actually not true that you can't take anything with you to heaven. You can actually take one thing. Do you know what that is?"

We all perked up. Even me. I had never gone to church a day in my life, but **EVEN I** knew that you can't take anything to heaven. Whether or not heaven existed, it seemed obvious that when you die, you leave with nothing. I was curious.

She stepped away from the podium and wasn't using the microphone anymore. We all wanted to know the answer, so we sat silent. She walked over and stood by the blanket girls and said, "People. You can take people to heaven with you."

She moved back to the podium and continued her point. "People, all people, are heavenly treasure. Even the kids at your school that you don't even like."

I had a headache. I didn't want to think about treasure anymore. No one ever talked like this. I could count on one hand the number of conversations I had had with anyone about God and heaven.

But she had one more thing to say. "Now that we know what Jesus meant by earthly treasure and heavenly treasure, I have a challenge for you all. Our scripture tonight talked about not storing up earthly treasure, and it ends with, 'Where your treasure is, there will your heart be.' So let's find out where our hearts are!"

She said this like it would be fun. "Your first challenge is to not buy anything for yourself for this entire month. No clothes, no downloads, not even extra candy or snacks at the vending machines. I'm calling it Project Treasure. Of course, you don't have to do it if you don't want to. That's why I call it a challenge. Those of you who are excited to try it are the ones who should do it."

Mrs. Belle said a prayer, but I didn't listen to a word of it. My brain still hurt from all of her foreign words. I wanted to argue with someone about all the claims she made about treasure and people and heaven. Who said there even *was* a heaven? Who said that having stuff is bad? Having stuff never hurt anyone. But when she said that ALL people were treasure, even the ones at school that I didn't like, that bothered me the most.

Lisa and the other ninth grade helpers waited at the door with a huge pile of fuzzy blankets for everyone. She tried to hand me one, but I rejected it, "I just watched." I said, "I didn't play the game, so I don't get one."

Lisa smiled and said, "Get used to it, Clover. Mr. and Mrs. Belle own a shopping network, and they are generous. She wants everyone to have these for comfort as they consider not buying anything for themselves this month."

I hesitated. I didn't want anyone to think that I agreed with anything that was said tonight.

"Take it, Clover. It's a gift." Lisa nudged the blanket into my chest, and I could feel how incredibly soft it was. I wrapped my arms around it and sunk my face into it. I couldn't help it.

"OH MAN that is soft!!!" I said.

"I know, right? Good luck with The Challenge!" she said and moved on to the next girl.

My mom was waiting for me in the lobby. As we were walking to the car, Mrs. Belle flagged us down and asked us to wait up. She was with the girl I'd seen sitting all alone in the back of Alpha Omega. The girl from the bus stop.

"Hi Maggie Ann," said Mrs. Belle. "Would you mind taking Sara home? She lives a couple houses down from you. I brought her here, but I need to stay later than I thought, so I can't take her home."

I looked at Sara and we smiled at each other. She seemed nice, and I wondered if she was just really shy.

"Sure we can do that," my mom said, "Which house are you in?" she asked Sara.

"Hers is the yellow house with the one-car garage, exactly two houses down from you," Mrs. Belle answered for her. Then she put her arm around Sara and said, "It will be good for you to go with them, Sara." Sara rolled her eyes and seemed reluctant to get in our car, and I wondered what was so wrong with me that she didn't even want to be in my car.

We drove home in silence. It was obvious that Sara didn't want to talk. My mom didn't ask me how the meeting was, and I didn't ask her why she left when she saw the bald girl, Lisa. We had a lot to think about, and I was mostly thinking about Sara in the back seat. She was definitely treasure, and I wondered what I would need to do to win her over as a friend.

When we arrived at Sara's house, she got out. My mom nudged me with her elbow to remind me to say goodbye. I squeaked out, "Bye, Sara, I'll see you at the bus stop tomorrow!" Sara thanked my mom for the ride. She shut the door and gave me a courtesy wave. It was far from friendship, but it felt nice that she acknowledged me.

The next day, I couldn't stop looking at people and wondering if they were treasure. When you're new, it doesn't take long to learn who the kids are that have labels. A girl in my math class couldn't seem to keep her mouth shut, and the whole school called her CSU, which stood for "Can't Shut Up." Was she treasure?

Things started to come together in English class when we talked about how to use irony in our writing. The teacher gave us some examples.

"You've all heard of the gentle and kind Manning Hitlery, who our town is named after, right? It's ironic that his last name is Hitlery because it reminds us of a person that we associate with the opposite of kind and gentle. Hitler was a terrible person, but Manning Hitlery is the opposite of that, so his name is ironic. Another example of irony would be a cop who spends his day writing tickets and then gets his own license revoked for getting too many speeding tickets. That's ironic."

The teacher, satisfied with her examples, said, "Okay, you try it now. Take about fifteen minutes to write a couple ironic statements of your own. Keep a list and add to it all year. You'll be incorporating all your ironic statements into your end of the year essay."

It was easy to write the first one. *The speaker who says that people are treasure and that worldly stuff doesn't matter owns a shopping network.* Yep. That was ironic.

The second one was more difficult. I thought about Mrs. Belle and her talk and about the girl, CSU, who talked too much. I also thought about my annoying brother. There was NO WAY he was treasure. I wrote: *The girl who doesn't believe people are treasure just bought $1,000 worth of stuff for other people when she could've bought it all for herself!* I shook my head and didn't care a lick if it was a statement of irony. Dumb Challenge.

I asked for a hall pass under the guise of going to the bathroom, but went to the lunchroom instead and bought a candy bar from the vending machine. I ate it all. Take THAT, Project Treasure!

Shipment

The whole month of September was a blur. I didn't want to go to Alpha Omega, but for some reason I couldn't live without it. I was a torn piece of paper about the whole thing.

I was so glad for my writing class because it gave me a chance to write about how I was feeling. I didn't really make a decision to use it as a journaling session. It just sort of happened that way.

One day our English teacher gave a lecture about using similes—when you say something is like something else—and we had to write an example. *When I go to Alpha Omega I feel like a splinter inside a finger that's connected to a huge body that I don't understand. An outsider...yet connected somehow. I don't belong, and yet I am stuck there. Maybe even causing people pain.* When she gave it back to me, I laughed. I got an A+ on the assignment about my heart feeling like an F. I'd have to remember to write that in my ironic file.

I rode the bus home with Twinkle on the last Thursday of September, and I complained about Alpha Omega that night.

For some reason she was amused by my angst. "Don't go if you hate it so much," she said, and I stared out the window feeling desperate.

"I was fine before I started going to Alpha Omega. Now I'm not fine. I think about weird things all the time," I vented.

"What sort of weird things?" Twinkle was curious.

"People! I think about people, okay? I never used to think about people!" My frustration was obvious.

"What did you think about before?" she asked, and I stared at her.

"Do you really want to know?" I asked. I wasn't sure she could handle it.

"Sure," she said, and I took a second to judge whether or not she would kiss our friendship goodbye if she knew the level of venom I really had for all this church stuff.

"Myself, Twinkle. I thought about myself. I thought about my stuff and how my room looks like a Troll doll wig factory!"

She laughed because she had seen my room and knew it was true.

"If I didn't want to talk to anyone, I didn't." I said. "I could buy a candy bar and eat it without thinking about it as worldly treasure. I could look at a kid at school like CSU ...." I looked around to see if she was on the bus and then started talking quieter, "I could look at a kid like CSU and not care. I didn't have to wonder whether CSU was annoying, or if she was treasure. My conclusion, Twinkle? It's that she is annoying! She is NOT treasure!" I looked at her to see what she would do. She had the most pleasant look on her face.

"Clover ... are you treasure?" her cheek was smooshed on the side of the bus seat. I didn't think it was gross, but I needed her to stop looking at me.

"Sick, Twinkle. Do you know how many greasy heads have pressed against that seat? Greasy *boy* heads?" I said, and she moved her face away real fast. I could tell I messed with her mind.

I was hoping she couldn't tell how much she had just completely messed with mine. The question of being treasure exposed the dark pit of emptiness that I liked to avoid and pretend wasn't there. I wanted to cry and shout and say, "NO! I'm not treasure! Maybe everyone else is, but I'm not!!!! Thanks for rubbing it in!!"

The bus let Twinkle off first, and for the rest of the ride home, I pressed my forehead against the window just as hard as my emotions were pressing against my insides. I got off at my stop, ran straight home, and into the bathroom. I locked the door, turned on the bathtub and let myself drown in how desperate and lost I felt. I wished I were pretty like Sara. I wished my mom wouldn't shut me out and run away every time there was a problem. I wished I were treasure. I couldn't remember the last time I cried that hard. When the bathtub was full, I got in and submerged my whole body under the hot water. Even my face. *Now I'm buried treasure*, I thought, and when I smiled it made a little bubble come out of my nose.

When I got out of the tub, I saw that I'd gotten a text message. It was from Twinkle.

Fundraiser stuff is here! she wrote.

I wrote back, *at your house now?*

She wrote, *Call me in 15. Chore time.* I couldn't wait to talk to her. I pictured the boxes all piled up in her front room. I couldn't wait to see it.

I walked out into the living room, and my mom was lounging back in her big recliner. She was reading *Seventeen* magazine. Give me a break. She's forty-one and still reads *Seventeen*.

"Hi Clovah. I'm taking a test to see what supah powah I would have if I was a supah hero. I'm almost done calculating the results. Let's see, I got mostly Bs so that means ... here it is, it says, 'If you got mostly B's, your supah powah is invisibility. You want to appear like you have it all togethah, but when it comes down to it, you don't want anyone to see ....'" She stopped reading abruptly, as though the analysis had gone too deep. "Do you want to take the test, Clovah?"

"No thanks, I already know what my superpower would be." She looked at me and raised her eyebrows as if to say, 'Well? Spill it?' Maybe her superpower was talking with her face.

"It would be X-ray vision ...." I answered.

I peered at her head like I could see what was underneath her wig. By doing that, I must have pressed some sort of button, "Go to your room, Clovah!!"

That command was out of the blue, so I didn't get up and go right away until she yelled again, even louder, "GO TO YOUR ROOM!!!"

I wanted to yell back at her, "What did I do wrong?" I wanted to shout, "Your wigs are stupid and embarrassing by the way!" but my instincts told me not to push it. I literally bit my lip in anger and went to my room and slammed the door. In the end, I felt sorry for her. She was obviously the one who was suffering some kind of mysterious consequence.

I called Twinkle and squealed, "It's all here?" I didn't even say hello.

"Yeah it's here. What did you buy, Clover? There are a lot of big boxes in my living room," she said.

"Maybe I could spend the night with you tomorrow and we could go through it? Judging by Rule #2, I have to give in secret, but that doesn't mean I can't show you. None of it is for you," I confessed.

"Gee, thanks!" She was fake disappointed.

That night I went to Alpha Omega and actually knew one of the songs we sang at the beginning. I still didn't sing, but it wasn't completely new anymore.

Sara was sitting by herself like usual, only closer. She was a couple rows back from us. That surprised me and made me wonder if she might be warming up to me. I almost went to talk to her, but I chickened out. There was plenty of time at the bus stop for social risk. I waved and said hello and joined Twinkle in our usual seat instead.

At the end of Mrs. Belle's talk, Lisa came forward wearing the cutest hat I'd ever seen. She had an announcement to make. "This year the catalog company is giving a prize to the person who sold the most stuff. This was a surprise to all of us." The entire room was buzzing.

"The winner is ...." My heart raced. I didn't want it to be me, especially if I had to go up in front of everyone. I hated that kind of attention. "... Clover Mannerhouse!" Everyone looked around to see who I was. My face got hot, and I squished down into my seat.

"Clover, you won! Get up and get your prize." Twinkle was an extrovert and didn't understand my need to be anonymous.

"Will you go get it for me?" I asked, but just as I said that, Lisa spotted me and said again, "Clover, you are the winner. Come up here and get your prize!" I didn't see anything up front or in her hand that would be mine.

Against my will, I walked to the front, and Lisa reached behind her and picked up the guitar that was on stage. I could hear the blood rush into my ears. I thought that guitar was for the person who led the singing. With a big grin on her face, she handed it to me. "What am I supposed to do with this?" I asked in Lisa's ear as she hugged me awkwardly around the guitar.

Mrs. Belle ended the meeting with me right up there in front of everyone. I stood terrified and held the guitar I would never use. Twinkle had her hands over her mouth like I had won the lottery.

When I finally met up with Twinkle, she was still in shock. "Luck---EEEEE!!!" she said like we were five years old.

"It's a guitar, Twinkle." I was not amused.

"No, it's more than that. You know all those songs on the radio station I showed you?" I gave her the tiniest shrug as if to say, 'Yeah, but I don't care.'

She threw her head back, "Oh this prize is so wasted on you!!! How did you win this??? If it were mine I would print off all those songs and stay up all night to learn them." She rolled her eyes like she couldn't believe how lame I was.

I set the guitar down to put my jacket on, and I noticed Sara looking at it like she wanted to play it. Something about her seemed familiar. She reminded me of the tall, slender girl that dressed in all black in the superhero movie, *The Incredibles*. Sara wore all black too. She didn't hide behind her bangs like Violet did in the movie, but there seemed to be something fragile about her.

My dad picked me up, and I put the clunky guitar in the back seat. When I got in the front he said, "Who's your friend?"

I laughed but didn't explain. It was probably rude to leave him guessing.

"No, really. Why do you have a guitar with you? Are we dropping it off at someone's house?" he asked.

I smiled. "No. It's mine."

"Ah. It's yours. Of course it is. You have no musical ear and no money to buy something like that. It makes perfect sense." His sarcasm was thick.

"I won it for selling the most stuff for the fundraiser. So I guess I will name the guitar *I'm Awesome.*" I was proud of my good comeback.

"You mean Mrs. Belle is awesome? She's the reason you won that prize." He had me there. I had nothing to say.

"I think you should name it Siberia because it will sit in the corner of your room getting cold and taking up space." My dad made clutter sound so dreary, and I immediately felt bad for all the stuff that was waiting for me at Twinkle's house for The Challenge.

My dad was right. I wasn't interested in playing the guitar. Maybe I WOULD call it Siberia.

The next night my mom drove me to Twinkle's. I took the guitar because she seemed to think she might have fun with it. Maybe I would accidentally lose it at her house.

But when I walked in her front door and saw all the boxes I ordered, I forgot about the guitar. I was completely blown away by how much there was. I had no idea the shipment was so large.

"Wow!" I said. It took over her whole living room.

"I know! What IS all this stuff?" she asked.

We opened the boxes one at a time, took the things into Twinkle's bedroom, and stored them in her closet. Everything was much smaller when it was unboxed.

"Five thousand glow sticks, Clover. Really? Out of that whole catalog you bought glow sticks?" We made a pyramid of the glow stick boxes up her wall because they didn't fit in the closet with all the other stuff.

"How am I supposed to know what *Be a light* means, Twinkle? It was the only thing in the whole catalog that I could imagine using to *Be a light*."

She looked at all the glow sticks and said, "I'm not saying it isn't going to be fun to use them. But five thousand? That's a lot."

I picked up the guitar and pretended I knew how to play it. Strumming without using chords, I sang a made up song in reply, "How's about you let me worry about the glow sticks ... Twinkle ... my little star ... and you ... you can have this guitar!" I stopped singing and said, "It's a little rodeo I made up just now."

"Rodeo? You mean a country song?" She laughed and I rolled my eyes. I was glad I didn't take myself so seriously and could laugh with her at my mistake.

I picked at the guitar while she went online to find some worship songs to print off and learn. For whatever reason, I remembered Sara right then and how she looked at my guitar. "Hey Twinkle, did you see Sara looking at this guitar when I set it down by her last night?"

"I didn't." she said. "Do you know her?"

"No, but I am so curious about her. We stand together at the bus stop, and she's nice but really cold at the same time. It's like she hates me AND likes me. It's really weird. I can't figure her out. I was hoping you knew her story. Maybe she likes music. Maybe she wants to learn guitar," I wondered out loud. "I've been thinking about giving it to her."

"Are you kidding me? You just got it!" Her body language exuded betrayal.

"You want it, don't you?" I smiled at her.

"Of course, I want it," she admitted.

I felt a bit of compassion for my friend. "Then you are going to be very mad at me because I've already made up my mind. If you had seen Sara's eyes when she looked at the guitar, you would make the same decision. She had a 'Twinkle' in her eye." I put air quotes around the word 'Twinkle' as I said it.

"Very funny, Clover! It's not like she isn't going to know who gave it to her. She saw you get the guitar. Remember Rule #2, *Give everything in secret?*" I could see she was trying to get me to change my mind. I didn't know why I chose Sara over Twinkle for the guitar. Twinkle was certainly a better friend. I guess that deep down, I was desperate for Sara to like me. If I gave her the guitar then maybe she wouldn't be so cold.

I ignored Twinkle's comment, so she got busy printing off all the worship songs. I handed her the guitar, "Here. You can have it for one night to make all your dreams come true, and then it goes away ... make it last ... and make it awesome."

She took the guitar and put the music in front of her. "How do you play a G chord?" she asked me, knowing full well I had no clue.

She fiddled around on the strings for about five minutes while I watched her. Defeated, she looked at me and said, "I say if Sara can figure this thing out, good luck to her!" She put the guitar aside and said, "Let's go online and find all the things we can do with glow sticks."

Give Everything
in Secret

*O*ctober in central California is a lot like every other month. Warm and nice.

I always wondered what kids in Alaska did for Halloween, where it is cold and dark and miserable. In Los Angeles it was warm and nice, too, but my mom never allowed me to go trick-or-treating because of all the crazies. She said it was just a small town thing. I planned on holding her to that now that we lived in Hitlery, the smallest town I could imagine. I didn't care if I was thirteen. I was doing it.

At the first meeting in October, Lisa walked up to the mic wearing a Jester's hat, which I thought fit her personality.

"As you know, Halloween is at the end of the month," she said, "and that's when we have our annual party at Mrs. Belle's house. We'll have games and go trick-or-treating together. And, as always, there will be a very competitive costume contest surrounding our theme. This year's theme is ... wait for it ... it's superheroes!!!"

There was a lot of creative excitement when she told us the theme. I guess everyone liked to think about dressing up as a superhero.

"Listen up!" Lisa said. "You need to know the categories for prizes! This year we have two categories, and they are: Most Creative Interpretation and Most Believable. You have a whole month to get ready, so have fun guys!" She waved and pranced off the stage and made the bells on her jester hat tinkle.

Mrs. Belle took the microphone and said, "I already have my idea for a costume. Great theme, planning committee!" We all kept whispering to each other—we were so chatty.

"If I could reel you all back to attention, we want to talk about our topic for October which is, *Give everything in secret.*"

Again, she caught my eye when she announced the topic. I was torn between yelling, "I get it, I get it!" and being thankful that she was spoon-feeding me the answers I needed to know. It was a relief that I wouldn't have to figure out The Challenge all by myself. I had a closet full of stuff at Twinkle's and no idea what to do with it. I didn't care about all the Bible stuff, but I did want to go to Disneyland.

She continued, "Our passage today is Matthew 6:1-4, which says, '*Beware of practicing your righteousness before other people in order to be seen by them, for then you will have no reward from your Father who is in heaven. Thus when you give to the needy, sound no trumpet before you, as the hypocrites do in the synagogues and in the streets, that they may be praised by others. Truly, I say to you, they have received their reward. But when you give to the needy, do not let your left hand know what your right hand is doing, so that your giving may be in secret. And your Father who sees in secret will reward you.*'/

"This scripture is about doing things in secret so that we don't focus on getting a reward from people, but from God. You could compare it to how you feel about getting attention. And girls, you know what it's like to want attention from people. I know you do."

She put her hand in her pocket and pulled out her phone and said, "Those of you who have phones, go ahead and take them out. Normally we discourage the use of phones, but right now it's alright."

She asked, "How many of you are on Instagram?" Most of the girls raised their hands.

"Go ahead and open up your account. Yes, I mean it, you can check your Instagram accounts right now." She had to prompt us a second time because we were so used to being scolded by teachers to put our phones away, rather than encouraged to take them out.

She scrolled away on her phone and asked us, "How many selfies do you think you have on file?"

We all started pointing and counting.

"Too many to count?" she asked.

Then she asked us to cover up our phones. "Without looking, tell me how many people follow you."

Several girls raised their hands. Mrs. Belle called on some girls, then checked their phones to see if they were right. I was having a great time with this conversation. I liked my phone and looking at my selfies and checking out who "liked" them.

"Oh man," she said, "we LOVE our phones and all the attention we get from it. We love it when our phones beep to say we have a text, and we love it when we get new followers."

Our heads were all down, our attention deep into our phones. She was talking, but we were half listening. "Girls it's time to put your phones away now." A collective moan rose up, and she waited until we put our phones down, which took awhile. We proved her point.

"Judging by how difficult it was for you to put your phones away, I think you would admit that you love the attention it gives you. It's like a reward. It's a way to be noticed, praised, complimented, and followed. Tonight's scripture doesn't talk about how we get attention from our phones, but how we get attention when we give money.

"Everyone reach under your seat. There is an envelope taped to your chair. But don't open it!" She said that a few times, so we wouldn't open it up and spoil whatever surprise was inside.

"When I say it's okay—not yet, but when I say so—please open your envelope, but keep what's inside a secret. Don't show anyone."

We opened our envelopes. Inside mine was a slip of paper that had $10,000 written on it with a black circle around it. She asked those of us that had a black circle to go up front. I wasn't going to do it, but then I saw that Sara was going up, so I decided to be brave and go stand by her. Twinkle gave me a big thumbs-up when I squeezed by her.

Mrs. Belle explained, "There's a number written on your piece of paper. Let's pretend that's the amount of money you'll give to the church tonight."

To those of us up front she said, "I'd like you girls to tell us what your number is, and you'll receive a reward from all of us. We'll stand up and clap for you, and then you'll get a present.

"If you are sitting down, please keep your number a secret. No one will ever know what you give. When the girls up front announce the amount they're giving, I want you to stand up and clap and cheer and make a big deal about it, okay?" She asked if anyone had any questions.

I didn't think it was such a big deal. I didn't know how this could make anyone feel special. It's not like I was giving $10,000 for real.

Sara went first. "I am giving $1,000," she said.

THE CHALLENGE *by Wendy Everts*

Everyone stood up and clapped, pretending to mean it. Mrs. Belle gave her a really cute hoody jacket with the number 1,000 on it. I had to admit, I was looking forward to my turn. I underestimated the emotional lift I felt when people clapped, and Sara certainly looked proud in her moment.

A couple other girls went, and then it was my turn. I announced that I was going to give $10,000, and the room erupted. I didn't know where to look. No one had ever clapped for me before, and I'm sure I turned bright red. Mrs. Belle gave me my own hoody jacket with the number 10,000 near the upper left shoulder. It was the coolest hoody I had ever owned. Lisa was right when she told me to get used to getting things from Mrs. Belle. She certainly loved to use her money to make a point.

I liked this exercise a lot better than the one where the phones were taken away. There didn't seem to be anything wrong, in my opinion, with getting attention from people, and I was glad I chose to go up front and risk embarrassment.

After we'd all had our turn, we sat back down and Mrs. Belle said, "We certainly saw how it felt to get attention from people, but let's hear from a couple of you who had to remain in your seats. How did it feel that you couldn't talk about what you gave?" Mrs. Belle asked.

One girl raised her hand and said, "I didn't mind clapping, that was fun. But when you gave out those cool hoodies, I wanted one too. I know it's supposed to be a secret, but I gave more than she did, and she got the jacket."

The other girls chimed in, "Yeah me too." They seemed to agree, and some even expressed anger at the process. I guess it would've been a pretend exercise, but the jackets made it real.

Twinkle left to go to the bathroom, and as she did, her paper fell on her chair. I noticed that it not only had a number, but there were words, as well. My curiosity got the best of me.

It said, *Your husband is dying of cancer. You have $100,000 in savings, but you decide to give $10,000 to the church and trust*

God for your medical bills, which will certainly be more than you have. I put the paper back on her chair.

I felt sick. I wondered how Twinkle felt that we both gave the same amount of money, but her sacrifice was bigger. The hoodie certainly made it seem real, and I was wearing one and she wasn't. I could be angry at Mrs. Belle for making me feel bad, except I was the one who looked at the paper. I wasn't supposed to know. Twinkle came back, and I tried my best to act like I didn't know that she deserved the hoody more than I did.

I wanted Mrs. Belle to say something to make me feel better. "We can either get attention from people," she said, "or we can get attention from God. The Bible doesn't say it's bad to get attention—it just challenges us to seek it from a certain place.

"When we get attention from people, it's immediate and it feels good. It's a reward that we feel right now. You girls who got the hoodies know that, don't you? But those of you who didn't get any applause or anything else had to sit there and learn what it feels like to wonder if anyone sees you. It's hard. We can't see God, so it takes a lot of trust to believe that he will take care of us, that he will make us feel good or give us the attention we need. That he will reward us in secret. Do you believe that?"

Her words hung in the air and landed in the pit of my stomach. No. I didn't believe that. In my universe, God didn't exist. My only option was to get attention from people.

Last month, I'd been preoccupied and almost obsessed with determining if everyone I saw was treasure, or in most cases, not treasure. Now I'd have to go home and wonder if there was a God. And if he DOES exist, how in the world would he give me attention? It's not like he was going to invite me to his birthday party or friend me on Instagram. I had never really thought about or cared if God was real. Maybe I still didn't.

Mrs. Belle prayed, and on our way out, the ninth grade volunteers passed out envelopes.

"Not again!" I said. "No more envelopes, please!"

Lisa laughed and said, "No it's good! There's a name inside for a Secret Santa exchange. It's The Challenge for this month. It's our way of giving everyone a chance to practice giving in secret." She was perky like always and excited for me to take the envelope.

I hesitated, so she asked, "What's the matter. Clover? You don't look like yourself tonight."

"I don't think I want to do it, Lisa." There was so much I could've said, but what I probably really wanted was a hug. I needed something to help me feel more a part of the group, not less.

"Taking this doesn't mean that you agree with Mrs. Belle or even believe in God. Think of it as a way to give someone the chance to experience what you did up front today." I wondered how she knew that I wasn't into the God stuff. Maybe it showed on my face.

I took an envelope and put it in the pocket of my brand new hoody. I went to the bathroom and read the letter. I figured that if I didn't want to do the Secret Santa thing, I could throw the envelope away in the bathroom garbage. No one would know it was mine.

The letter said:

> The Challenge this month is a Secret Santa Exchange ... with a twist!! Inside this envelope is a name, and during October, November, and December, you will do special things for her, but you'll do them in secret. The twist is that, in December, there won't be any reveal. You won't ever tell your person who you are. We are going to practice getting attention from God instead of people.

I wondered who my person was, so I looked in the envelope. Nothing there. I turned the paper over and there it was: *Betsy Belle.*

I sighed. Not her! What would I give her? She had everything. And then I realized that if she already had everything, then I didn't need to do much. She was already getting her reward from God, right? She didn't need me to give her much attention. Perfect. I put the paper back in my pocket.

My mom picked me up and asked me how it went. I shrugged and said, "Good, I guess."

My mind wandered, trying to come up with ideas of what I could get Mrs. Belle. It was mildly entertaining and a bit of a waste of time to think about what to give a woman who already had everything. I wondered how the other girls were going to get money to buy their presents. They'd probably ask their parents for money, something I would never do.

Without thinking I said, "Actually we're doing a little project, and I might need a way to earn some money." It wasn't really a question. My mom didn't say anything—which wasn't really an answer, either.

That night I lay in bed and looked at my piece of paper. There was something else written under the name *Betsy Belle*:

> *Bless the name on this paper in secret. Remember that sometimes the best blessings in life are free. Pray for her and love her, using your own personality and gifts. Be creative and have FUN!!!*

I was pretty sure I didn't know how to be a blessing. That word didn't mean anything to me. The only thing I knew about blessing someone was after they sneezed. Maybe I should give her a bunch of tissues?

I tried to quiet my brain and get to sleep, but I heard a car stop outside our house. A car door opened and shut, but no one knocked on our door. My mom was up—probably making my yearly ornament—so the lights were on in the living room. Why didn't they knock? I wanted to let it go and just fall asleep, but I couldn't. I kept thinking about the note.

The note said I could pray for her. No I couldn't. I didn't know how to pray. I said out loud, "I don't even believe in you, so how can I pray?" I waited to see if I would be struck by lightning. I thought about all the prayers Mrs. Belle said after her talk and the prayers the guitar players said in between their singing.

Just for fun, I orchestrated a fake prayer for Mrs. Belle that mocked every prayer I'd ever heard at Alpha Omega, "Dear Father God, give Betsy Belle open eyes to see thee more clearly. Open her eyes, and open her mouth and open her ears, and open her nose, and open her doors, thou thou thou thee." I played around with my voice.

No one at Alpha Omega had ever said the words "thou" and "thee," but in my mind they seemed like good ridiculous religious words to use in a mocking prayer.

My mom woke me up the next morning, which meant that I'd actually fallen asleep at some point. It was earlier than usual.

"Good morning, Clovah," she said as I mumbled a sleepy, "What time is it?"

She completely ignored my question and said, "I emailed Mrs. Belle last night to see if she had any work you could do, so you could earn some extra money."

"You what?" That woke me up. It was the last thing in the world that I wanted. If I worked for Mrs. Belle, then she would be giving me HER money. She might as well buy herself her own gifts.

"You heard me, Clovah," she said. "I told her you wanted to earn some extra money for some Alpha Omega project." I moaned out loud and buried my head in my pillow. She had just ruined it.

Ignoring my body language, Mom said, "She was thrilled that you asked, Clovah, and said she would love to help you. She has a dog you can walk every morning if you want, and she'll give you five dollars a day."

I perked up and said, "Five dollars a day for walking a dog? That's a lot!"

She was smiling. "I know, Clovah!"

Maybe it wasn't going to be so bad after all. I could walk a dog for five dollars a day. Even if I did it during the week and not on the weekends, that would be $25 a week. I was doing some serious math and liked the ending sum.

"I woke you up early so you could go over before school. She said you could start this morning if you want to get over there around 6:40."

"What time is it now?" I asked.

"It's 6:30. You have plenty of time. You can walk the dog, then shower and get ready for school aftah," she said.

I put on my sweats and got ready as quickly as possible. When I opened the door, I saw a present sitting on the porch. It had my name written in big words on the top, 'To: Clover Mannerhouse.'

"Oh my gosh," I said out loud.

"What is it, Clovah?" My mom was at the table eating cereal and reading *Seventeen* magazine. She already had a full face of makeup and her wig on at 6:30 a.m. Unbelievable.

"It's something for me." I put the gift on the table and couldn't believe that someone had already given me something. I had completely forgotten one thing about this whole Secret Santa thing—someone out there had my name as well.

I was afraid that I wouldn't make it to Mrs. Belle's house by 6:40 and said, "I'll open it when I get back." I ran out the door but turned around and said to my mother, "Don't you dare open it."

She looked at me so offended and said, "Clovah, why would I open your present?" I didn't hear her finish because I ran out the door to earn five dollars.

Walking the Dog Club

I ran to Mrs. Belle's house. Her living room light was on, and behind the screen door, her front door was open. She was expecting me.

"Good morning, Clover," she said. "Let's go around back, and I'll show you how to take the dog out without my help. That way you can come over any time you want to and take him for a walk."

"Okay," I said.

Mrs. Belle was in her sweats, too, and she looked like she had just gotten out of bed. I always thought that she didn't wear any makeup, but it was obvious now that she did freshen herself up. She looked more ashen and plain, and her hair was ratty.

She saw me staring at her and said, "Oh, Clover, I must be a mess the way you are looking at me!" I was embarrassed that she noticed.

"Oh no! It's just ... I'm sorry, but I've never seen my mom look like you do now and ... I'm sorry I'm staring. I'm surprised that you are letting me see you this way. I mean, you look great. I didn't mean to say that you look bad. You look real. Like a real person."

She looked at me with sad eyes that I didn't understand, then changed the subject. "Come with me," she said. We went to the backyard, and she showed me how to open the gate from the outside. She introduced me to her dog. She said he was high-energy, and even though she took him for walks, he needed a lot more exercise.

She gave me the leash and showed me how to be in control when I walked him. We practiced a bit around her yard, and it was hard at first, but I learned that when he started to pull on the leash, I needed to pull him back toward me to let him know that I was in charge.

After my lesson, we sat on the backyard bench and watched the dog run around. Every once in a while he trotted over for affection.

"Why don't we just stay in my yard today?" Mrs. Belle suggested. "Then if you want to walk him tomorrow, you can. Or you can wait until Monday if you want to sleep in this weekend. I am up every morning to spend time with God, so it doesn't matter to me."

"You get up early, even on weekends?" I asked.

"Yep." She said it like it was normal.

"Adults are strange," I said.

That tickled her. "I suppose we are. Sort of like how your mom never lets you see her like this?" She took her hands and messed up her hair even more. It was sticking out all over, and I was embarrassed for her.

"No," I said, "I'm used to my mom. YOU are the one that's weird." I was joking, but in all seriousness, I did think Mrs. Belle was different.

She sighed and said, "I've been called worse, much worse." I couldn't imagine anyone calling her anything worse. She was weird, but pleasant weird.

"I should probably ask you a question since we have time," I said. I wanted to talk to her about giving the guitar to Sara. I didn't know Sara very well and thought maybe she could give me advice about whether or not she would like it.

Mrs. Belle didn't say anything but patiently waited for me to continue. "I really appreciate the generous gift of the guitar. I don't know who donated it, but whoever it was doesn't know me well. There really isn't anything I can do with it."

I felt hesitant to say that I wanted to give it away. I didn't want to hurt her feelings if she had something to do with the gift. I'd never talked to anyone about serious things. At least this felt serious. It was more than just giving the guitar to Sara. I wanted to know if she thought Sara would receive it from me or if she would reject it.

I looked down at my lap and said, "I just need to get this out and say it: I'd like to give the guitar to Sara, but I don't know how to do it. I don't know if she would want it from me."

"Oh is THAT all? Gosh, with how you were acting, I had no idea what you were going to say. That's a wonderful idea!" she said, obviously relieved.

"When I won the guitar at Alpha Omega, I set it down right by Sara, and she looked at it like she wanted it. I figured that she would get more enjoyment out of it than I would," I explained.

Mrs. Belle looked thrilled and nodded as if I had the right idea about her.

I decided to share my insecurities about my friendship with Sara. I needed to know more about her. It would affect how I gave her the guitar.

"The problem is, I don't know if Sara likes me. She is nice to me at the bus stop. We say 'hi' to each other, and when I ask her questions she just answers with one word. She never says more or asks me any questions. I figure she has enough friends maybe?" It was a rhetorical question that I was hoping she'd answer.

Mrs. Belle smiled at me—sort of—again. It was the same sad smile she gave me when I told her that I never saw my mom without a wig.

She sighed deeply and said with resolve, "Sara is really shy, Clover."

It was something I wondered about but never understood. "Why would she be shy? She's so beautiful. Everyone wants to be her friend." I didn't know that for a fact, I just knew that I wanted to be her friend.

"I know," Mrs. Belle agreed. "I tell her that all the time."

She was quiet for a minute, and it seemed like she was holding something back. I was about to ask her what was wrong, but she looked at me with great concern and started to speak before I could. "Sara had a best friend that lived in the neighborhood, Clover. They did everything together. Their mothers were even pregnant at the same time, and so Sara and her friend knew each other since they were babies.

"As they got older, they walked back and forth between their houses all the time. Last year, her friend moved away. Her father got a job in Washington State, so she moved at the beginning of the summer.

"Sara was crushed. She's having a tough time this year because, not only is she missing her friend that was like a sister, she's had to learn how to make other friends for the first time."

"They must have lived close," I said, "if they walked back and forth like that. Where did her friend live?"

Mrs. Belle hesitated. She answered gently, "She lived in your house, Clover."

My chest tightened. "Oh," I said. "No wonder."

"No wonder what?" Mrs. Belle asked.

"No wonder she doesn't like me." It all became clear. "She's mad that her friend moved and I took her house."

Mrs. Belle was quiet. "Give her time, Clover. You are right that she is angry, but it's not about you, it's what you represent.

You remind her of how much she misses her friend. But do keep in mind, she DOES need friends."

Mrs. Belle smiled and put her hand on my back.

"She's making progress. I could see that when she moved to sit behind you in Alpha Omega. She'll be alright. I think the guitar is a great idea. She sings all the time and loves music. Keep trying to be her friend because that's the way to go through life. No matter how people treat you, assume that everyone wants to be your friend in due time."

I wouldn't have guessed that a girl like Sara could feel alone or could hurt so badly. I thought beautiful people didn't have any problems because they looked so put together. Even though I felt doomed by the very nature of where I lived, I felt better to know that there wasn't anything wrong with me. I liked what Mrs. Belle said, "Assume everyone wants to be your friend in due time."

"Just give her time and keep trying," she reminded me.

Now that I knew Sara's story, I was confident that giving her the guitar—in secret—was the right thing to do. I didn't want her to think I was manipulating her into being friends with me. I would need Mrs. Belle's help.

"My idea is to give the guitar to you," I said, "and you can give it away at the Halloween party as a prize for the best costume. No one will know it's the same guitar, and you don't have to tell Sara that the costume contest was already decided." I hoped Mrs. Belle liked the idea.

"Clover, that's a great thought. But ...." She hesitated and I wondered what the problem was.

"But what, Mrs. Belle?" I asked.

"Even if she comes to the party, I can't imagine her wearing a costume. I've known her all her life, and she wanted to dress up for Halloween until about third grade, but then she stopped. Sara is incredibly artsy, so the guitar is a great idea. But she seems to think that dressing up is childish, and I just can't see her showing up in a costume. That girl is unpredictable, I tell you." Mrs. Belle looked skeptical. "And she really is shy. I wasn't making that up."

Sara was certainly a mystery. She was artsy and yet wore plain clothes, all black. She was shy, but she went up front during the exercise in Alpha Omega. The fact that Sara was inconsistent made me determined to not give up on the costume idea.

Maybe it would work out to make a way for her to win the guitar, and maybe it wouldn't. The point was to give it to her. Mrs. Belle could easily do that without me being involved.

"Why don't I give you the guitar. If she shows up at the party and is dressed up, then she wins the prize. If not, then you can give it to her at the end of the night. Either way, she gets it and doesn't know it's from me."

Mrs. Belle put her hand out and said, "Deal." We shook on it, and she said, "Look at the time! You'd better get going! It's 7:20, and you have a bus to catch at 8:00."

When I walked in the door, my mom put down her magazine. She had a panicked look on her face. "Thank God you're back, Clovah. I'm dying to see what's in this package. Open it. Open it!!"

I unwrapped the gift, and inside was a beautiful Bible. A Bible? Really? All that excitement for nothing. "It's a Bible, Mom. Knock yourself out." I slapped it down on the kitchen table and went to get ready for school. This wasn't Secret Santa, this was Secret Frickin' Jesus! I probably wouldn't get anything good out of this ridiculous game.

"What'd you say, Clovah?" my mom asked.

I stopped and turned toward her. I didn't realize I'd said anything out loud. "Nothing."

I got ready for school and went out to eat breakfast and, who would believe it, my mom was sitting at the kitchen table looking at the Bible. I stopped dead in my tracks.

"Are you reading that thing?" I asked.

"Sort of. I'm just skimming it mostly. Betsy asked me to do a Bible study with her. I'm just checking it out to see if there is anything worth my time. I haven't decided if I want to do it yet," she answered.

I didn't say anything and neither did she. It looked like she had found something to read that was worth her time. I made myself a bowl of cereal, sat back at the table, and watched my mom. She looked like a square peg trying to fit through a round hole.

"There is a big difference between that Bible and *Seventeen*, Mom. I'm not sure it's at your reading level." I was joking, but only halfway. I didn't think she could handle the adult content. I didn't say it, but I thought she might have to grow up a bit.

"I don't know, Clovah, listen to this." Out of that whole book, she just happened to open it up to a story that was just like *Seventeen* Magazine. She read the unbelievable words about a girl who got months of beauty treatments before she went to see some king. "I don't know what's in the rest of this book, Clovah, but I like this one called Estah. I'm gonna ask Betsy what kind of beauty treatments they used on this girl."

I laughed inside thinking about my mom having a Bible study with Mrs. Belle. She would probably make it into some kind of magazine quiz. I almost said that they should have the Bible study at our house, in case she needed to run away to cry or take a bath when things got too deep. She had NO idea what she was getting into.

I opened the door to head for the bus and she said, "Oh, Clovah?"

"Mom, I'll be late for the bus. What?" Our street was pretty flat, and I could see that the bus wasn't coming yet.

"Dad said that Mr. Belle invited him to church this Sunday, and he wants us all to go toogethah." As always, she dropped that little 'Mom bomb' right as I was heading out, so I couldn't argue about it. I rolled my eyes and ran to the bus stop.

Sara was there alone, as usual. I was feeling a little more confident after talking to Mrs. Belle. I knew Sara's story, and Mrs. Belle's words were still ringing in my head. *"Keep trying to be her friend because that's the way to go through life. No matter how people treat you, assume that everyone wants to be your friend in due time."* I figured I would go ahead and talk but wouldn't expect her to respond. Like Mrs. Belle said, *"Give her space."*

"Hi Sara." I said.

"Hi," she answered. This was our normal morning routine, which usually ended there.

"My parents want us to all go to church this Sunday. I am so mad," I said.

She looked at me and smiled but went right back to staring at her phone. I took the risk and told her that I didn't grow up in church and that Alpha Omega was really new to me. I told her that I didn't understand what Mrs. Belle was talking about most of the time.

I saw the bus coming up the street.

Then I really went out on a limb and invited her to walk the dog with me in the mornings. "Hey so ... I am going to walk Mrs. Belle's dog in the mornings. If you want to walk with me, you can."

Sara took a deep breath and blew it out like she had something heavy on her chest.

"I'll be going by your house every day at 6:40. We'll go as far as Twinkle's house and turn back. If you aren't out, then I'll know you aren't interested, okay?" I tried to be as friendly as possible, though I was terrified by what I'd just done.

Thank God the bus was here. Perfect timing. Great distraction from the invitation I just gave her.

School was uneventful. Lots of kids were talking up their Halloween costumes at lunch. In English class I added another simile to my list: *Thinking about going to church feels awkward and hard, like hiking up a hill on a gravel road wearing roller skates.*

On the bus home, I sat across from Sara, and when I got off I said, "Remember, Monday morning 6:40, if you want to join me!" I tried to be like Lisa, who made everything sound fun. I hoped I wasn't being obnoxious.

The weekend seemed to drag on and on. That church thing. I went through my closet and tried on at least twenty outfits I might wear. Nothing looked right. Even my favorite clothes looked dumb. It was like my insecurities leaked out and made my clothes look stupid.

Sunday morning came soon enough, and the Mannerhouse family was a sight to see. My dad looked like he was going to work. My mom looked like she does every day, but when my brother and I came out of our rooms both our parents stopped and stared. "Who died?" my dad asked. We were both wearing black and had our shirts buttoned all the way up.

"What?" we said. We lifted our hands up in surrender and said, "We don't know what to wear to church! We've never been to church!" We were a chorus of unknowing.

Our parents didn't have any suggestions about how to fix our appearance, so we all piled in the car and left.

Before the service started, Twinkle came over to sit by us. My brother looked at her and said, "What's up, Twitter?"

"Hashtag, good one!" she answered.

That put him in a giggle fit that you could hear across the entire church for the first five minutes. My mom popped her gum as loud as a woodpecker pecks until my dad finally put his hand in front of her mouth so she would spit it out. To put the icing on the cake, my dad belted out the second verse of a song before it actually started. Other than that, we were perfectly incognito and completely unnoticeable.

On the way home we were pretty quiet, but when we got inside my dad said, "Well. We lived—and I didn't hate it. I'd go again."

We all moaned and collapsed on the couch, even my mom. My brother complained that he'd given up an hour and a half of his life that he would never get back. I didn't know what to say.

That night, I set my alarm for 6:30 a.m. and laid out my school clothes, so I could be as quick as possible getting out the door.

Just like she said, Mrs. Belle was up and had let her dog out in the backyard. I put his leash on him, gave him some hasty affection, and we were on our way. I didn't know what to expect. Why did I ask Sara to join me?

We were right on time. If Sara wanted to come, she should be waiting outside. It was fairly light out, but because she always wore black, I couldn't see if she was there or not until I got close. I fully expected her not to show up, but to my surprise, there she was.

"Hi, Sara," I said, trying not to sound too shocked.

"Hi," she said back.

She clutched her phone like it was her security blanket, but for the first time ever, she didn't look at it.

I didn't expect her to say much, so while we walked, I told her all about our move to Hitlery and how my mom had sprung it on me that I had to go to Alpha Omega. Even though the route to Twinkle's house and back was a full twenty minutes, I had no trouble talking the whole time. It felt good to talk. I actually enjoyed telling her my story.

When we got back to Sara's, I said, "See ya' later alligator. Thanks for letting me talk."

She lifted her hand and said, "Bye." She got halfway through her yard and turned around and said, "Oh yeah, Clover?"

"Yeah?" I answered.

"Are you going to the Halloween party?" she asked.

"Yep! I'm excited for it."

"Okay, good." She turned around and walked inside.

I smiled. Maybe Sara liked me! I skipped down the street.

The house between ours was decorated for Halloween and had a graveyard with fake bodies coming halfway out of the earth. *Those bodies are like my heart,* I thought. They were like the part of me that felt dead and unlovable, but now they were waking up and coming out for new life. Loveable life.

I said in my best horror voice, loud enough for the neighbors to hear, "I'm Alive … I'm … ALIVE!!!"

The Costume

My alarm went off the next morning at 6:30, and I was eager to get up and earn five more dollars. I was also eager to tell Sara my idea for a Halloween costume for her. Even if she decided not to wear it, it was a great idea, and it would give us something to talk about.

Sure enough, when I got to Sara's house, she was waiting outside. The day before, I hadn't expected much from her, so I felt pretty confident. After she asked me if I was going to the Halloween party, I thought I detected a hint of friendship.

As she walked toward me, I started to get nervous. Sara was gorgeous, intimidatingly beautiful.

"Hey, Sara," I said.

"Hey, Clover."

Today felt awkward. I didn't know what to say, and she clearly wasn't the most talkative person in the world.

I wanted to talk to her about the costume, but before I sprang the idea on her, I thought it would be good to have some small talk. I had to start with something.

"Mrs. Belle has a nice dog," I said.

"Yeah," she said back. I had hoped she would say more than one word. Twenty minutes together was a long time.

"Have you known Mrs. Belle for very long?" I asked.

Sara laughed and looked at me. "She's my grandma!" she said, surprised that I didn't know.

"She is? I didn't know that!" It was such an obvious thing, now that I did know.

I studied her a little more closely, like people do when they are trying to find the family resemblance. "Oh yeah, your eyes do match hers a little bit."

"You should see our baby pictures," she said.

"Are they alike?" I asked.

"Yeah." She answered in her typical one word way.

"I'd like to see them sometime," I offered.

"You can," she said. "All our family pictures are up at the Millie Hitlery Hotel."

"Why are they at the ...?"

I was about to ask why *her* pictures would be *there*, and then the words on the hotel menu came back to me:

> *When the couple died, their house was given to their one and only daughter. She turned it into a hotel and held a national essay contest to give it away to a worthy couple. The only thing the daughter insisted on was that the hotel be named after her mother, Millie Hitlery, because that's what her father would have wanted.*

"Your great-grandparents are Manning and Millie Hitlery!" I shouted. "And Mrs. Belle was their one and only daughter. She would've totally given that hotel away. She is so generous!" The connection was obvious and also gave me greater insight into how Sara could be so quiet and yet carry herself with such great confidence.

Sara smiled. I could tell she was proud of her family roots, and I was glad we had something we could talk more about. And since we had reached a new level of comfort with each other, I decided to go for it with the Halloween costume idea.

"By the way, I have an idea for a costume you could wear to the Halloween party."

Sara frowned and was about to, I'm sure, say that she stopped dressing up years ago, but I didn't give her the chance. I pretended that dressing up was a mature thing to do and that she would love it.

"I've been thinking about how much you look like that girl from *The Incredibles*. You know, the one who is real shy? You HAVE seen *The Incredibles* haven't you?"

"Yeah I've seen it, but ...."

I interrupted her so she couldn't go on.

"It's a good movie!" I said. "And you look just like Violet, because you wear black and have black hair that lays across your face just like hers. All you need to do is wear a little name badge that says 'Violet' and people will go nuts! You'll be the best one there, and you don't even need to do a thing. Think about it, okay?"

She was thinking about it, I could tell. It was almost like she was fighting some inner turmoil. She bit her lip, she was thinking so hard. I was just glad she didn't refuse altogether.

"I will even make you a name badge if you want," I said. "You wouldn't have to do anything. Will you think about it?" I tried to seal the deal.

"I'll think about it, but don't get mad if you show up with a name tag and I don't wear it okay?"

"Cross my heart!!" I said, probably a little too enthusiastically.

I spent the rest of our walk being glad that the awkwardness with Sara was over. I talked about the different superheroes and the pros and cons of dressing up like them.

When we got to her house, she summed me up. "You wonder a lot, Clover," she said.

"Then maybe I'll be Wonder Woman!" I said. It was settled. That was perfect.

Of course, I couldn't think about the party without thinking about Twinkle. Because she always gave me a thumbs-up, I knew exactly who she would be too. I had it all figured out. If she agreed, that is ....

The Halloween Party

I had told Twinkle all about walking the dog with Sara, and sometimes she would watch for us out her window. She'd wave and sometimes she would come out and join us for the walk back. It took a bit for Sara to get comfortable with Twinkle, but in due time it happened, just like Mrs. Belle said.

Halloween happened to be on a Friday, and we were super psyched about it. Twinkle came over after school before the party. We had each decided to go for the Most Creative Interpretation prize.

Twinkle liked my idea for her costume and had gone shopping to get a couple of things: a big foam hand in a thumbs-up position and a stretchy cap that looked like an old man's bald head. Whenever someone came up to her at the party, she planned to stick out the giant thumb and say, "SUPER!!!" The perfect Superman.

I, on the other hand, was going to attach quote bubbles all over me that said various things like, "I wonder how many stars are up in the sky?" and "I wonder who I will marry?" The perfect Wonder Woman.

We thought we were hilarious.

The party started at 5:00.

Twinkle and I got ready in my bedroom, and on our way out my brother saw Twinkle. "Hey, Twilight!" he said.

He had just read the Twilight series and was obsessed with vampires. So much so that he put holes in things all around our house to make it look like he'd bitten them with his fangs. All our bananas had two punctures in them, a fang apart. Very juvenile for a sixteen-year-old, if you asked me.

Twinkle reached into her pocket and stuck some plastic fangs in her mouth, "Thank you for finally changing me, Ryan!" she said, as though my brother had bitten her and turned her into a vampire too. Only with the oversized fangs her words were muffled, and slobber poured out of her mouth.

"I can't believe you had those fangs in your pocket," I said.

She seemed just as surprised as I was. "It was a Halloween miracle!" she declared, and we both laughed.

I really liked the fact that she was so quick and witty when people teased her about her name.

We headed to Sara's house. I had told her we'd meet her at 4:45 so that she wouldn't feel pressured to dress up ahead of time with Twinkle and me. I had made her a *Hello My Name Is* name tag with the name *Violet,* and underneath in parentheses I wrote (*The Incredibles*) because I wanted to be sure people knew she was a character from the movie.

She was waiting outside for us as usual. She looked perfect. She was slender and wore a plain black T-shirt and straight leg black jeans. Her bangs were combed to the side and fell in her eyes, just like Violet in the movie.

I held out the nametag, "Do you want to wear this? You don't have to if you don't want to."

I waved it in front of her face as if to hypnotize her. After about fifteen seconds, she actually groaned and grabbed it out of my hand, like she was surrendering to some kind of torture. I shot Twinkle a quick look of surprise.

"YESSSSS!" I said.

Twinkle put her big old foam thumb out and said, "SUPER!!!!" Then she said, "Get it, Sara? I'm Superman?"

Sara nodded and said, "Just don't be 'Stupid Man,' or I won't want to be seen with you. I hate dressing up, it's so silly!!!"

I stuck the name tag on Sara, then shouted, "Hands in the middle, girls!" like we were going to do a team cheer before a big game.

I didn't think Sara would join it. She was already stretched pretty thin with just the nametag. Reluctantly she put her hand in the middle, and both Twinkle and Sara looked at me for the next move. The problem was I didn't have any witty chant ready, so I came up with something lame.

"Awesome superheroes ready for a good time at a party!! Go! Woo hoo!" I tried to act like it wasn't a stupid thing to say, but it was. I shook it off by saying, "Rookie move—sorry." They just laughed.

Mrs. Belle greeted us at the door. She hugged Sara immediately. When she saw her name tag she said out loud, "Violet? You are Violet from *The Incredibles,* Sara? That is genius! You look just like her!" Mrs. Belle looked at me as if to say, "I don't know how you did it Clover Mannerhouse!"

The three of us pretty much stayed together the whole night. I had gotten to know some of the other girls by sitting together at lunch, so it was fun to see them outside of school.

Lisa was there with the other ninth grade volunteers, and they had set up activity stations all over the house that kept us busy. You could travel to a different activity whenever you wanted. We spent the most time at the craft stations. All three of us loved that. There were girls packed inside the house and out. It was super fun.

Before we went trick-or-treating, Lisa gathered us together and said, "We have one last thing to do before we disperse in groups to trick-or-treat. I know some of you won't come back afterward, so we want to announce the winners of the costume contest now.

"You all went above and beyond this year. It was a great theme, although I don't think Dora the Explorer is actually a superhero, am I right?" We all looked at the girl who had dressed up as Dora and laughed. She put her hands up as if to say, "My bad!!"

"We'll start with the Most Creative Interpretation prize." Lisa said. "There were a lot of creative interpretations this year, and I just want to highlight a few. Wonder Woman is wondering and Superman is super, do you agree?"

Several girls applauded and squealed in delight for our efforts. "But the most creative interpretation this year goes to … drum roll, please!" We all patted our laps to drum up the suspense. "Spider Man!" We all cheered and had expected that the girl who wore a mustache and had little plastic spiders crawling all over her would win.

"And now for the winner of the most realistic costume." Lisa got real serious. "This time we have an actual prize for the winner of this category. Evidently it's the year of the guitar because this is the second guitar we've given away."

She held it up. I noticed Sara was holding her breath.

"Many of you tried to look like your favorite superhero, and I was impressed with the fake muscle costumes."

When she said this, all the girls who spent a ton of money on their store-bought costumes started flexing to show off.

"But we have someone who beat you all hands down." We all drummed on our laps without a cue.

"The Winner is Violet from *The Incredibles*!" The whole room erupted.

Mrs. Belle stood right beside her, as if to provide a layer of protection from all the attention, although Sara didn't need it. She looked strong and confident. She didn't seem as fragile to me as she did the night she sat in the back at Alpha Omega. Maybe being shy wasn't what made Sara fragile. Maybe it was the sadness of missing her friend. Maybe now that she had warmed up to us, I would get to see a new side of her.

"Ladies," Mrs. Belle said, "I know you're anxious to head out for trick-or-treating, so no acceptance speech from Sara tonight. I'll get the guitar to her a little later. Why don't you break into groups and head out together. No one goes alone okay? Some of you have permission to walk home afterward, and some of you need to come back so your parents can pick you up here. You know who you are. Now go have a good time!"

I assumed that we would go out as a group of three, but I was wrong. Sara had left us. I saw her sitting at the table with Mrs. Belle, holding her new guitar in a playing position. She stroked the guitar gently while Mrs. Belle looked on.

"It looks like she might know how to play a G chord," I said to Twinkle. I didn't know what those words even meant but thought it would be funny to bring up that night that we were lost when the guitar was in our possession.

"Sara is definitely not up for trick-or-treating. I think we better get going before the group leaves." I pulled at Twinkle to head out the door.

"Yeah, but let's go congratulate her first." Twinkle pulled me harder toward Sara. I hesitated because all the girls were leaving, and I didn't want to miss my opportunity to fill my pillow case full of peanut butter cups and Snickers.

We went to Sara and I said, "Good job, Sara. Thank you for using my idea. I thought it would be great."

"Hey, we could play duets!" she said.

My face froze, and I didn't know how to tell her there was only one guitar.

Thankfully Mrs. Belle heard us and came to the rescue. "Sounds good to me. If you ever want lessons, Clover, I will make that happen for you. Just say the word and I could get you what you need." She winked in my direction. I could tell that she was encouraging Sara in her friendship with me and also letting me know that if I needed to get another guitar, she would get it for me.

Twinkle added, "Good job, Sara. See you later."

With that, we went outside to live out my childhood dream of begging for candy. The whole street was packed with kids and families. It was easier than I thought to find a group of girls from Alpha Omega to join.

Trick-or-treating was even more magical than I imagined. All I had to do was knock on a door, and candy spilled into my pillowcase. I ate every piece I got from the first five houses, but soon realized I couldn't keep that up. There was simply too much.

I looked at Twinkle and said, "I like living here." She lifted up her foam thumb, said, "SUPER!!!" and gave me a cheesy smile. I loved that girl.

Be a Light

 had earned a whopping $75 walking Mrs. Belle's dog in October. Now I had to figure out how to use the money to buy something for her.

So far my Secret Santa had given me a Bible, and I had no clue who she was. Maybe that's all I would get from her. Or maybe I should say, that's all my mom would get, since she was the one who actually used it. Who knew my mom would become quite the little Bible study girl?

We still had another month to play Secret Santa, and I thought I would save up my money and get Mrs. Belle something big at the end. Maybe a bird feeder? No. Too practical.

At the next Alpha Omega meeting, Mrs. Belle introduced the topic for November, *Be a Light*.

To create an effect, she turned all the lights off and shut all the doors to make the room pitch black. There weren't any windows, so the room was very dark. She told us to look at the person next to us. I tried to look at both Twinkle and Sara on either side of me, but all I could see was black, thick and dark.

She asked, "How much light do you think you need to see the person next to you? Just think about the answer, don't say it out loud. Do you think you would need to turn on a lamp to see them? Or do I only need to light a tiny match way over here? Would that tiny light in this great big room be enough?

"Let's try it. I'm going to light this match, and I want you to notice how much, if anything, you can see. You won't have much time before the match burns out, so pay attention!"

She fumbled with the matches, and we heard a strike. We looked around the room and couldn't believe it. That match didn't make everything bright, but we could see the glimmer of every face in the room.

There were lots of "whoa's" and "ah's," and the light went out. Like she said, it didn't last long.

Someone turned the overhead lights back on, and we squinted and moaned, as though we'd been in the dark forever.

Mrs. Belle talked about the Bible verse of the day, which was a short one, thank goodness. I wasn't really listening. At the end she said that the purpose of light was to illuminate and expose the things in the dark so that we could see clearly. Then there was something about Jesus being the light for us, but I didn't get that.

I had five thousand glow sticks to use for The Challenge this month and, of course, this was the one message I didn't understand. Great. Just great.

"That was so awesome!" Twinkle said.

I looked at her, confused, "What was so awesome about that? I didn't get any of it."

"The world is dark, Clover, and we are lights. We can make a difference! We can change the WORLD!" She was so excited that I thought maybe I should give her the five thousand glow sticks so she could use them to change the world.

"Wow," I said. "Clearly you know something I don't." I was underwhelmed.

Twinkle left to talk to the girls that sat with us at lunch. I leaned over and said to Sara, "I guess Twinkle needs to talk to people who understand. I wish I could talk to someone who doesn't understand. Am I the only one here that doesn't buy this Jesus stuff? Am I the only one with questions here?" We sat in silence. "I don't get it. I just don't."

After a minute, Sara looked straight ahead and said, "It's okay, Clover."

She seemed timid and distant, as though she didn't really know what to say, but she was trying.

Her words were spot on. I needed to hear that it was okay. More than that, I needed to know that I was okay. I remembered the first time we walked. I talked and talked about my life. Probably out of desperation for something to say, but hadn't she listened? After my monologue about my life, she took the initiative and asked me about the Halloween party. Sara wasn't afraid of the fact that I didn't have faith. I repeated her words over and over in my head. "It's okay, Clover." Almost like those words were from God himself.

For some reason, I couldn't get up to leave. Sometimes being in a room full of people can be lonelier than being all by yourself, especially when you feel like the odd man out. I watched as the girls grouped together like a school of fish swimming in the same direction. I wondered what it would be like to swim with them. I wondered what it would be like to say that God is real and to believe everything, like they did.

Twinkle rejoined us, "Hey Wonder Woman! You guys are in a quiet mood!"

I thought it was witty that she called me Wonder Woman. Could she tell from the look on my face that I was thinking? That I was, indeed, wondering? Maybe that was coincidence.

All of a sudden, Sara looked fidgety and wrong. Her face muscles were contorted and she looked uncomfortable. I could see sweat on her upper lip.

"Sara? Are you okay?" Her skin looked grey and ashen, and she seemed to be in a panic. She rocked like she was nervous and she grabbed her hair with her hands. I asked her again, "Sara, are you alright?" Every second that went by was more urgent. She seemed to have slipped out of reality.

"Twinkle, get help!" I yelled, "Someone! We need help! Mrs. Belle!"

Mrs. Belle stopped her conversation and ran over to us. I broke out in a sweat, and felt like if I got up my legs wouldn't hold me.

"Sara, Sara," Mrs. Belle called. "Can you hear me? Stay with me sweetie, Grandma has your pills. You're going to be fine."

She reached in her pocket and pulled out a bottle. She opened it and put a big purple round thing in Sara's mouth. She had one hand on Sara's face to keep the pill in her mouth and her other arm was wrapped around Sara's body.

She looked at us and said firmly, "Why don't you girls go to the lobby and pray for her. We'll talk later and I'll answer your questions. She'll be fine."

Suddenly, my feelings of being different were gone, and we were all united with love and concern for Sara. The few girls that were still at Alpha Omega left the room, and I ducked into the bathroom to gather my wits. I hadn't realized how tense my body was. I was weak and nauseated. I wanted to lay down. I wanted to go home.

When I came out, my dad was looking for me. He took one look at the group gathered in the lobby praying and then at me and knew he needed to get me out of there. He held my hand as we drove off, which was really sweet.

"Rough meeting?" he asked.

I told him that Sara was sitting right next to me and how scary it was when her body started getting weaker and she didn't respond. He listened with concern. When we got home, he led me to my bedroom and said, "Put on your pajamas and brush your teeth, and I'll tuck you in. You've had a big night."

I was emotionally exhausted. I got into bed and my dad was right there. He pulled the covers up to my neck and combed my hair with his fingers. "You know it's alright if you need to cry."

That was it. Those words of permission opened the floodgates, and I started sobbing. He got the tissues and was a pro at not saying anything. He just let me cry.

After I was done I looked at him and said, "You're a good cry friend, Dad. Have you done that before?"

His eyes were distant and sad, like a man who wished he could've lived a different life. He gave no answer but just put his hand lovingly on my face and wiped some tears away.

I slept hard that night.

In the morning, I didn't want to walk the dog. I did, however, want to talk to Mrs. Belle about what happened last night. I wondered what I would've done if that had happened while Sara and I were walking the dog.

"Sara has diabetes," Mrs. Belle said as we sat in her dining room. She had made me some tea, which was nice. Apple cinnamon tea smells good when you've cried yourself to sleep.

"She always carries her glucose pills with her, and she can usually get to them before there's a problem. Last night, it came on very strong. That can happen when there's a change in her diet or with excessive exercise."

My heart dropped. "You know that Sara has been walking the dog with me, Mrs. Belle? Everyday. Is it my fault that she got sick last night?"

"Oh, I doubt it, Clover," Mrs. Belle put her hand on my shoulder. "Walking for fifteen minutes in the morning isn't what you would call excessive exercise. And I assure you that if walking with you gives her low blood sugar attacks, then it's worth it. Being your friend is changing her, and I can tell that you are filling a much needed void in her life. You will never know how much you have blessed me by being a friend to Sara."

She could barely say the last part without crying. I couldn't help but feel selfishly proud that I was filling a void in her life.

She answered more questions and told me the signs to look for that would indicate Sara needed to take a glucose pill before things got too bad. I could remind her to do that.

I was nervous to be alone with Sara, but Mrs. Belle said she would meet me at the bus stop this morning so that she could break the ice between us and put my fears to rest. I was grateful. I wanted to still be Sara's friend, but I was scared something like that would happen again.

It was time to get ready for school, and as I walked out the door I said, "Thanks, Mrs. Belle. I'm not going to walk the dog this morning, but I think he'll understand." I was wrong. He greeted me at the door, wagging his tail like he was expecting a walk.

"Or maybe not," I said and we both laughed. "I want to send Sara an invitation to my birthday party, so she knows I'm not afraid of her." It wasn't true, but I thought it was an important thing to do. After last night, I realized that Sara was a good friend, and I didn't want to lose that just because I was scared.

"That's a great idea, Clover," Mrs. Belle said. "Please keep shining your light. It's working."

I didn't respond to that. I waved and walked home while I thought about her words. She said I was "blessing her so much by being Sara's friend" and to keep "shining my light." I noticed that she couldn't talk about Sara and me without tearing up. She called me a light and said that what I was doing was working.

What was I doing? I had no clue what she was talking about. I was relieved that without even knowing it, I was holding my end of the Secret Santa bargain. I was doing what the card had asked me to do. I was giving something to Mrs. Belle. Even though I didn't understand it. Score!

Go, me.

Birthday Party

I didn't know if Sara knew that everyone had seen her diabetes attack the night before. In our house we never talked about anything, so I figured we would pretend it never happened. As promised Mrs. Belle was at the bus stop, and I was so glad.

"Hi Sara," I said.

"Hi. Sorry I scared you last night," she said.

"That's okay." But it wasn't, and I started crying, which was a surprise to myself. She hugged me and I hugged her back.

"I sort of thought you were dying, and I didn't know what to do." I laughed nervously.

"Yeah. Sorry about that. I'm okay though now, see?" and she slapped her face and did a jig. It was a weird thing to do, but it broke the ice. I guess we were both feeling awkward.

Mrs. Belle looked at her as if to encourage her to say more, but she shrugged and let it go. Whatever it was, she didn't want to say it and I didn't care. After last night, I was glad to see that she was okay.

The next morning we walked the dog. Sara took out her glucose pills to show me they were in her pocket, just to assure me that she had them. That put me at ease and I joked, "Great, you brought the dog treats. Good to know where those are in case we get hungry."

I took a risk in being sarcastic. I wasn't sure how to be myself in this situation. I put my arm around her shoulder and, to my surprise, she relaxed. She was nervous too.

My birthday party was all set for Saturday, November 15. Twinkle, Sara, and I went to my favorite pizza place. My mom let my brother drive us, which made me feel so grown up to go out without parents. Even though Ryan stayed the whole time and ordered food to eat at another table, we still felt like we were alone. Our only disappointment was that he didn't sit closer, so we could chuck straw wrappers at him.

Twinkle took out a present from her bag, "Here, Clover. We got you a present from both of us. We pooled our money, so we could get a better gift!!" Sara seemed calm and comfortable. We were all less nervous since her episode had been a couple of weeks earlier.

It was a fairly large present—a huge makeup kit with several different colors of eye shadow and blush, applicators, and lip gloss.

"Wow you guys. This is awesome! Best gift EVER! Let's go home and watch YouTube videos and experiment." I said.

"YESSSSS!" Twinkle said with a fist pump.

Sara nodded, "I have a tutorial that I watch all the time. I already know what I want to try."

We literally stuffed our faces with pizza, then the sirens went off and five of the wait staff surrounded our table. They plunked down a dessert in front of me that was ablaze with candles. Twinkle and Sara laughed and clapped along with their birthday song. I rolled my eyes and pretended to hate it, which was code for I loved it.

"Happy happy birthday, happy happy day! We wish you kind-ness, happiness, and joy in every way. HEY!"

It was like listening to the cheerleading squad at a football game. Not genuine, but at least they put some energy into it.

All the way home we sang diva girl songs and tried to make the car rock at stop signs. My brother hated that and tried to go as slow as possible as he approached red lights, so he wouldn't have to stop. We tried to rock the car anyway.

At home, there was a package on my doorstep.

"Ooooooh looky, Clover, another present!" said Twinkle. I had already told her about the Bible. She started to reach for the present to bring it inside.

I quickly grabbed her shoulder and said, "Wait! I don't want my mom to know about this. She might steal it like the last pre-sent. Let's take it inside, and we can open it in my room."

We walked in and saw that my mom was snuggling with my dad on the couch and watching old recordings of Funniest Home Videos. They were cracking up.

"Did you girls have fun?" she asked.

"Hiya, Mr. and Mrs. Mannerhouse!" said Twinkle.

Sara smiled then noticed the TV. "Ooooooh I love America's Funniest Home Videos!" She started to sit down, but I grabbed her fast.

"Nooooo! We're going to hang out in my room!" I said and encouraged both girls away from my parents and the TV.

The present on the porch was a photo album, and it had a picture of me from Los Angeles on the front.

"No way," I said. "How did someone get this picture?"

We all read the words on the front aloud. It said *My Jour-ney*. Inside were pictures of me with my family, with my school friends, and at Alpha Omega events. There was also a picture of me getting the guitar and one of the three of us at the Halloween party. Only a third of the album was full, and there was a note inside that said I could add pictures from the rest of the year.

"I thought this was from my Secret Santa, but who would have pictures of me in Los Angeles *and* now?"

"What about your Instagram account?" asked Twinkle.

"I thought of that, but these pictures aren't on it," I said.

"That's strange," said Sara.

"Did YOU give this to me?" I asked Twinkle.

"No," said Twinkle. I gave her a look that implied that her 'no' was unconvincing. She raised her hands up and said, "I swear on my dead and buried American Girl doll that I had nothing to do with this present!"

Sara and I stared at her. "You have a dead and buried American Girl doll?"

"Yeah," she said. "The worst part is that we left her in a box in the ground at our old house in Colorado. If the family that lives there now does any digging, they will find her. I hope they don't creep out." She said all this like it was no big deal.

"Wait, wait, wait ... You buried an American Girl doll in a box in the ground?" We gave her "the face." The face that demanded an explanation.

"I was seven years old, and I had a cat named Not So. His real name was Nacho, but I couldn't say that when I was two, so I called him Not So and it stuck." Twinkle was looking in the mirror and putting on eye shadow while she talked.

"My hippie parents loved that and made it our house joke. They always used his name like the beginning of a sentence and then finished it. They would hold him on their lap and say, 'Not so fat!' or if he would shirk food they would ask, 'Not so hungry?' Like I said, they adored that joke.

"I had an American Girl doll, too, and when I played with both her and the cat, it was like they were real humans you know? They kept me from being so lonely as an only child."

I got up and said, "Okay hold on, you have to see this." I interrupted her story to show Twinkle and Sara my childhood doll. Her name was Natalie and I put her on the bed with us to participate in our girl time, "Alright, go on."

"Not So was a sweet cat, and my parents always said he would live a long time because we kept him inside. I didn't know how much I counted on that until he got out one day and darted into the street. He got hit by a car." She stopped putting on makeup and looked at us with an exaggerated sad face. Sara and I sat still.

"Not So cool," I said.

"Not So cool is right!" agreed Twinkle. "I was only in the first grade and had never dealt with death before. Especially something so sudden.

"The next week my American Girl doll got really sick and every day she got weaker and weaker. That Saturday morning my mom found me in my bedroom sobbing and holding my doll. I was yelling at her, 'Why did you have to die? Why? Why?'

"The funny thing is that my mom ended up taking me to a psychiatrist! HA! I bet not many kids have been to a psychiatrist!"

Sara chimed in, "I have."

"What?! You too?" Twinkle asked, surprised.

"Yeah, but go on. You tell your story first." Sara patted her knee in encouragement.

"Okay, so, anyway, the doctor told my parents that my American Girl doll had died a slow death because it was my way of processing grief. He said that Not So had died suddenly, and I needed closure—closure that they hadn't provided. He suggested they take me seriously and do something to give me closure with my doll. So they got a box, and we put her in it and had a service to bury that doll. I cried and cried and said good-bye to her."

She paused, "And then I was over it. I guess the psychiatrist was right." She said all perky. "THAT is why there is a dead American Girl doll buried in my old backyard in Boulder, Colorado."

THE CHALLENGE *by Wendy Everts*

"That was strangely deep and wise and creepy all at the same time," I said.

"Yeah," Twinkle said. "Now you go, Sara. Why have YOU been to a psychiatrist?"

"Yeah, Sara. What did you bury in YOUR backyard!?"

She laughed, "Nothing. I started wearing black two years ago. It was about the same time I was diagnosed with diabetes, and I guess my parents wondered if I was all right. They were afraid I was going Goth or something," she said.

We waited again. When she didn't say anything else, I asked, "What happened?" I started trying on lipstick to lighten the mood. I wasn't sure if there was something seriously wrong that we didn't know about. With Sara anything was possible.

"The doctor met with me and my parents for a consultation. He asked them about any changes in my behavior, but my parents had nothing to say."

Sara spoke slowly and took her time.

"What did your parents do?" I asked.

"Nothing," she said. "All they said was that I had started wearing black and there were no other changes."

"What did the doctor say?" I asked.

She smiled. "After a while he stopped asking my parents the questions and looked at me. He said, 'Sara, why are you wearing black these days?' and I said, 'I think it's classy and I love the way it matches my hair.'"

Twinkle and I smirked out loud. Parents just don't understand what it's like to be a teenager. I could totally see her at the psychiatrist's office being mature and practical like that.

She pushed her bangs out of her face and showed us her makeup job. She had used black eyeliner and dark eye shadow, and her blue eyes popped like two giant sapphires.

"Wow, Sara! Your eyes are amazing!" Twinkle said. She was so pretty that I couldn't stop staring at her. I wished MY eyes popped like that. I looked in the mirror and tried to be satisfied with my face. It was hard to be friends with Sara because I was always jealous of everything about her.

Just then my mom barged into my room. It was like she expected to catch us doing something boring, and she was going to save the day by being the super-fun mom.

"Hey girls!!!" she said, way too trying-to-be-cool-like. "It's 10 o'clock, the party is ovah! I told your parents I would take you home, so you don't walk in the dark."

"Wow, Mom, you just made my inner twenty-one-year-old feel fourteen again. Thanks for that."

She handed us some makeup remover to use before she drove my friends home. I wasn't sure how she knew that we were all dying to get that unfamiliar mask feeling off our faces at that exact moment, but she did. It was moments like those when she anticipated my needs like a mature forty-year-old that my mom really impressed me.

After they left, I took out my photo album again. I stared at the words *My Journey* on the front and wondered what that was supposed to mean. I used my fingernail to test the letters to see how securely they were glued, and I found I could pull them up fairly easily. When I had time I would pick them off and replace them with the year instead. That was something I could understand.

Love Your Enemies

At the first Alpha Omega meeting in December, Twinkle leaned over and said, "When are you going to use all the stuff you bought that's sitting at our house? It's already December, Clover!"

"I have a plan," I said avoiding eye contact.

"Do you have a plan?" she was calling my bluff.

"No," I admitted.

Sara laughed. She'd overheard our conversation. She knew about The Challenge and had seen all my stuff at Twinkle's house.

Sara looked especially beautiful. Her hair was curled and she actually wore makeup. Her clothes were still all black but were particularly trendy and artsy. Her blouse had a beautiful neckline that framed her face and she wore skinny jeans with boots that slimmed her even more.

"What's the occasion?" I asked her.

"What do you mean?" she asked.

"You look really beautiful tonight." I touched her hair because it looked so fluffy. She karate chopped my hand gently and said, "No touchy!" I laughed.

The worship team fired up the music, and after three months, I pretty much knew all the songs and sang them like an old pro. I had no intention of ever singing, except they buttered me up with a silly song called, *'Chase that bird that's flyin' over thar!'*

At our second or third Alpha Omega meeting, the worship team started strumming their guitars and making 'caw' sounds. The girls stood up and whooped and clapped like they knew what was about to happen. I, on the other hand, had no idea what was going on. During the chorus a couple girls ran around like they were birds, and during the verses, some the girls chased after them. It was totally random and exhilarating to watch girls my age chasing each other. I laughed out loud and found myself singing along. Lo and behold, when the worship songs came after that silly song, I sang along with those too. I didn't even know I was doing it.

By now, I knew that the monthly theme would have something to do with The Challenge, and I looked forward to it.

"This is December, so the new theme is *Love Your Enemies*," Mrs. Belle said. "I am going to jump right in because we have a lot to do this week."

I noticed some furniture and large items over to the side, and big sheets covered something up. I wondered what that was for. I renewed my personal commitment to not volunteer for anything.

Mrs. Belle read from the Bible as usual, "Matthew 5:43-48 says, *'You have heard that it was said, you shall love your neighbor and hate your enemy. But I say to you, love your enemies and pray for those who persecute you, so that you may be sons of your Father who is in heaven. For he makes his sun rise on the evil and on the good, and sends rain on the just and on the unjust. For if you love those who love you, what reward do you have? Do not even the tax collectors do the same? And if you* greet only your brothers, what more are you doing than others? Do not even the Gentiles do the same? You therefore must be perfect, as your heavenly Father is perfect.'"

At the sound of the words, "Be perfect," I groaned and whispered, "Well I'm out!"

Twinkle whispered, "Shhhh!" but Sara laughed. That was the second laugh I got from Sara that night. I was feeling pretty funny.

Mrs. Belle was animated, "Tonight we are going to talk about what it means that Jesus invites us to be perfect. It's a pretty intimidating thing!

"I have asked the ninth grade girls to prepare a skit. Hopefully this will be a light and funny way to show you what I think goes through your heads when you hear the invitation to be perfect. Girls? Are you ready?"

She took the podium off with her, and all the ninth grade helpers came in. A crew of them started to grab the stuff that was off to the side. They didn't use all of it; there was still something under the sheet.

To the left, they set up a bunch of boxes in a rectangle and placed a quilt over the top. In the middle they put a table with four chairs. On the right, they put a desk like you would find in a girl's bedroom and another small table and chair. The moving crew was done, and we were looking at three separate skit stations.

Lisa walked in wearing grown-up clothes. Another girl came on stage with pajamas. She laid down on the boxes and put the blanket over her. I figured that she was the kid and Lisa was the mom.

Lisa came in and said softly, "Good morning, sweetie!"

The girl sat up without complaining and rubbed her eyes and reached her arms up to stretch. "Good morning, Mommy!" Her voice was syrupy sweet. We all grumbled out a mocking laugh. No one I knew got up like that.

"I made you eggs and toast. Please remember to make your bed before you come out to eat." Lisa put her hand on her daughter's face and then lovingly poked the tip of her nose. The daughter smiled, comforted by the gesture.

"Okay Mommy! Thank you for all that you do for me!" The daughter got up, chipper and ready to obey. She was smiling as she made her bed.

I shifted in my seat. This was exactly what I thought Christians were like. Happy all the time and obedient, like robots that didn't think for themselves.

Lisa and the girl left and four more girls came out with backpacks. They sat around the table in the middle and took out fake lunches and started fake eating.

"UGH! I look so ugly. I'm totally having a bad hair day!" one girl said.

"Nuh uh," said the girl sitting by her. "Your hair looks awesome. My hair looks dorky, it's sticking out everywhere. I hate it!"

"No way, your hair looks great. I'm so embarrassed about my outfit today. My mom told me I had to do my own laundry and I didn't have time. It's all her fault that I had to wear these jeans. They make me look so fat!"

While the girls carried on about their looks, Sara got up. At first I thought she was going to the bathroom. She'd been sitting on the edge, perfectly set up to sneak out quietly without disturbing the skit.

To my surprise, she wasn't discreet at all. She walked tall and proud with a glide worthy of fashion week in New York. I almost asked her what she was doing, and then I realized she was part of the skit. The girls around the table said, "Oh, my gosh, here comes Sara. Look at her, she's PERFECT. She is so skinny. She thinks she is better than all of us, I bet. A girl like that would never want to be our friend. I wish I had that body. She could be a model."

The girls said out loud everything that I thought about Sara. I remembered that in the beginning, I didn't think she would want to be my friend because a girl that pretty must have dozens of them. I compared myself to her all the time. Especially when we put on makeup at my birthday party.

My feelings had changed when I learned how much she was hurting and that she missed her friend. I felt different when I found out that she was lonely, not stuck up. She needed people to be nice to her, not judge her. Sara had more than outside beauty. She was a good listener and was funny. She didn't ever talk about other people behind their backs. I wished the skit would be over, that they would stop talking. Even though I was friends with Sara now, their words showed me how ugly it was to judge someone based on how they appeared on the outside.

Sara walked by the girls, and they got up and followed her out. The next crew of actors came on the stage. A girl sat down at her desk with a notebook. She was obviously studying.

Another girl who pretended to be her mom said, "Hey Barbie! We are going to the movies. Come on! We're going to be late." I wondered if they used that name on purpose or if that was actually the girl's name.

"Aw Mom, I can't. I have to study!" Barbie whined.

"But you've been studying all weekend. Surely you can take a break."

"I CAN'T!" Barbie got mad. "If I don't get an A, then they won't put me in advanced placement next year. If I don't graduate high school with advanced placement, then I won't get scholarships, and I won't get into college. Everything has to be perfect, Mom! I ... have to be PERFECT!!!" The girl who played Barbie started crying. Real tears. It was impressive. And powerful. I never put that kind of pressure on myself, but some of the girls at the Alpha Omega lunch table did. Some of them studied at lunch. I looked around to see how they were responding.

She cried for a while and the girl playing her mom stood by her with her hand on her back. We all had time to watch them and think about the three scenarios: sickeningly fake obedience, body image, and achievement. Sara had slipped back in the room to sit by us again, but I didn't look at her. I couldn't. My heart was heavy with guilt.

Mrs. Belle came up front. While she talked, the girls at the desk left quietly. "I'm letting the ninth graders teach tonight. They have learned a lot about what it means to be perfect. The scenes you just watched were real ways that these girls struggle with the image of perfection. Now they will show you how Jesus has changed them and what it really means to be perfect."

She stepped aside while the girls took down the props. They took everything away except for the desk, which was over to the side. They draped a white tablecloth over it and a girl stood behind it wearing an apron. She looked like a coffee barista.

Another girl came forward and read from the Bible, "*But I say to you, love your enemies and pray for those who persecute you.*" She stepped out of the way.

Then a group walked in together, laughing and talking. Lisa sat at the small table, reading a book and minding her own business. She looked fine. There wasn't anything wrong with her that I could see. When the other girls noticed her, they stopped walking. "Be quiet! She'll hear you." They giggled some more. They were obviously making fun of Lisa, but she did her best to ignore them.

The girls laughed again and whispered loudly, "She probably stays home by herself and reads every Friday night just for fun. I bet she dies alone."

Lisa stopped what she was doing and looked at them.

"Shhhhh, she can hear you!" one of them said.

Lisa walked over to the barista. I figured from the scripture reading that one of the mean girls would wise up, leave her group, and try to make friends with Lisa. These stories were so predictable.

Lisa pulled out a big wad of money, like she was paying for something. The barista put seven coffee cups in cardboard trays. Lisa picked them up and turned around.

No way, I thought. Was she going give the coffee to those girls?

"Here," she said to them. "I want you to have these." The group didn't make the scene cheesy. They seemed genuinely touched.

"Why would you do that?" one of them asked.

She shrugged. "Just wanted to," Lisa said as she walked off. "Have a nice day."

The girls seemed stunned. They started to walk off stage, holding their cups, when the barista shouted, "Hey girls!"

They stopped and looked at her.

"That was all the money she had!"

That was more than a skit, I thought. The twist at the end surprised me. I thought for sure someone from the group would go apologize. But Lisa made the first move, which was interesting.

When the skit was over, Lisa walked back in with the other girls and stepped up to the microphone. The girls surrounded her, arms around each other.

"So ...." I could tell Lisa was trying not to cry. "This skit was sort of about me.

"Last fall when I found out I had cancer, I was really low ... the kind of low where you get depressed and don't want to get out of bed. I came to Alpha Omega as much as I could. I had to go to a lot of treatments, and I lost my hair.

"They said my hair would grow back about three months after I went into remission, and I looked forward to that. That spring I started to gain back some weight and look normal, but my hair never came in. The doctors didn't want me to worry, but they said that, for some people, it could take years to get their hair back."

"You're beautiful, Lisa!" her friends behind her said in support.

She smiled, "Thanks guys."

She continued. "The month that we focused on *Love Your Enemies*, Mrs. Belle said that to be perfect, we needed to love hard people. That didn't mean anything to me until one day, my mom and I went to the mall. She left me to read a book in a coffee shop while she shopped."

She handed the microphone to one of the girls behind her and linked arms with the others while the new girl talked.

"I'm not proud of what I'm about to say," she said. She looked back at the group, and they nodded as if to urge her on.

"I was part of this group of girls behind me, and I led the pack to make fun of Lisa that day. She was just reading her book, and it was obvious that she didn't have hair. We were all hyper that day and weren't thinking. Maybe we wanted to do something that made us feel better about ourselves. We did and said those terrible things to her."

Lisa started to cry, remembering that day.

"I'll never forget what it felt like when she spent all her money to buy us that coffee. We sure deserved something, but we didn't deserve that."

The girls all went to the side of the room where the last prop lay and pulled off the sheet. They lifted a heavy wooden cross that was underneath and placed it on the desk, then opened a desk drawer and took out a hammer.

Lisa took the microphone and read Matthew 5:44 again, *"But I say to you, love your enemies and pray for those who persecute you."*

Each girl was handed the microphone, and one-by-one they each confessed what they had done to Lisa, right in front of her. Twinkle and Sara were both crying. I didn't want to, but it was coming from my gut and I didn't know if I could hold it back. I didn't know if I should leave. I got up and stood in the back, so I could cry in private. I wanted to see. There was something inside me that craved that closeness of the room.

The first girl said, "Lisa, I ran up and tore the hat off your head so that you would be bald in public, and we could make fun of you." She took the hammer and nailed a nail into the cross.

The next girl said, "Lisa, I hid your hat so that you couldn't find it." She hammered another nail into the cross.

The pounding was loud in my ears. I didn't know what it meant to put a nail in the cross, but it felt right. I had a yearning to go next and say, "Sara, I judged you for being so beautiful. I thought you were too arrogant to be friends with someone plain like me." I wanted to pound a nail too. What was happening to me?

As each girl took her turn, Lisa hugged her and said into the microphone, "I forgive you."

When they were all finished, Mrs. Belle came forward, her eyes filled with tears. She blew her nose and wiped her eyes. What a weird thing it was to see a grown woman who wasn't afraid to show her tears.

With a loving tone, she gave us an invitation, "The Challenge for this month is to *Love Your Enemies*. When we do that, it's perfect love, because that's what Jesus did for us on the cross. Perfect love. Jesus didn't die for us when we do the right thing like make our beds and get good grades. He died for us when we steal a bald girl's hat ...."

It seemed harsh, but we laughed.

"He died for us when we steal something from our brother's room and then lie about it." We laughed again. I may or may not have done that.

"He died for us ...." I finished her sentence in my head ... *when you judge your friend for being beautiful.*

She motioned to the ninth graders, and they came forward and passed out paper and pencils. I wiped my face with my shirt and sat back down.

"I want you to do two things with this paper. First, think about the skit. What people in your life are hard to love? Don't write their names. Just write down whether or not you will be nice to them like Lisa was when she bought the coffee. In the end, that turned out well for Lisa. But it doesn't always go well.

"I don't care what you write on your papers. Just be honest with yourself. Will you accept this challenge? Will you love as Jesus has loved you?"

It didn't take me long to think about the people who were hard to love. At the top of my mind was CSU, little miss Can't Shut Up. There was also a girl everyone called "Robocop" because she walked around school and tried to make everyone follow the rules. There was my mom who was crazy and, of course, my brother.

Would I love them like Jesus loved me on the cross? I wrote the words that pounded over and over in my head while Mrs. Belle's was talking.

I scribbled them in large capital letters with three exclamation marks:

IT'S TOO MUCH!!!

"What's that all about, Clover?" Twinkle asked.

I stopped scribbling and said, "I think I get the cross thing ... and I'm freaking out!"

The room was suddenly hot, and it felt like people were staring at me. "I need to get out of here," I said and walked out. I waited outside in the fresh air until my parents came to pick me up.

Sara

The next morning I walked the dog. Sara met me as usual. I was quiet.

My heart was heavy.

Last night I felt like the rug had been pulled out from under me. I'd never heard anything like that before. I had never seen people openly cry and share and tell each other deep things, embarrassing and shameful things.

Hearing those girls confess what they had done opened my eyes to something different. I felt like I was outside a house, looking in at a family who knew how to really love each other. I wasn't ready to enter the house yet, but then again, I didn't want to go back to where I was before. I had questions. I was scared.

I wanted to talk about it, but I didn't know what "it" was, so I said nothing.

"You're quiet today," Sara said.

"Yeah. I have a lot on my mind."

"Wanna talk about it?" Sara asked.

That was my cue to spill it, but I didn't know where to start. She had sat by me a couple weeks ago when I talked about not understanding and feeling so alone. But then she had her blood sugar episode, and I didn't even know if she remembered that conversation.

"Well if you aren't going to talk, I will," she said. "Last night was oddly powerful. I don't think I've ever understood the cross. It's never been explained to me like that. It was almost too much."

"Wait. I thought you were a Christian," I said.

"Yeah, well, sort of," she answered.

"How can you be a *sort of* Christian?" I wanted to know. Maybe I could be that too. Maybe I could stand in the doorway and just look in.

"There are things you don't know about me, Clover. I haven't had a strong faith in the past year. Just because my Grandma is Betsy Belle doesn't mean I believe in God."

I felt uneasy. She didn't know that Mrs. Belle had told me everything. I was so consumed with my own questions that I hadn't realized that Sara might need to talk too. I didn't see it coming that THE Sara Belle might not believe in God.

"You don't believe in God?" I asked shocked.

"No, I do, I'm just saying, don't assume. I don't like it when people think they know who I am just because my Grandma is the leader at Alpha Omega." She seemed feisty.

I was scared to say anything else because I didn't want her to be mad. I felt like everything I said was wrong.

"It's just that ... last night all that honesty made me feel like **YELLING**!!!" She bent down and picked up a rock and chucked it hard.

"What do you want to yell about?" I asked.

Sara picked up another rock and yelled, "**I HATE IT THAT MY BEST FRIEND MOVED AWAY!!!**" She chucked the rock and picked up another one.

"I HATE IT THAT PEOPLE DON'T TALK TO ME BECAUSE THEY ARE INTIMIDATED BY HOW I LOOK!!!" She leaned way back and chucked the rock as hard as she could. My stomach rolled over, remembering the skit from last night and how I had been part of that problem for her.

"I HATE IT THAT I FEEL LIKE I HAVE TO BE A GOOD EXAMPLE BECAUSE MY GRANDMA IS BETSY BELLE!!!" When she bent down to pick up another rock, she started crying.

She was too upset to keep going, so I picked up a rock and threw it as hard as I could. The rock smacked into the ground only five feet in front of us. Luckily it didn't hit the dog. She laughed and cried at the same time. It did look silly. I laughed too.

"You suck at throwing rocks," she teased.

"Oh yeah?" I bent down to get another rock. There weren't many on the side of the road. Chunks of gravel would be more accurate to describe what we had to work with. This time, I found a twig that looked heavy enough to throw and chucked it high, being careful to throw it up and not down this time. The twig wasn't dense enough. We watched as it sailed high, then landed on the dog's backside. He was startled but not hurt.

"See?" Sara said.

I finished her thought before she could say it, "I DO suck at throwing rocks!!"

She took in a deep breath and cleared her emotions. She was done. We walked together in quiet. Instead of dropping Sara off at her house, we sat on her porch together.

"I don't know what it feels like to be you, Sara." I said.

"And I don't know what it feels like to be on the outside of the church your whole life and hear what we heard last night," she replied. "I know you have so many questions. I know you feel lonely at Alpha Omega. That must have been so confusing and emotional for you."

So she DID remember the night that I told her I didn't get it. She knew me. I didn't have to say anything.

"I want to tell you something, Clover. It's going to sound bad, but it ends well okay?"

"Okay," I said reluctantly.

"There was a girl who lived in your house, and she moved away last summer. We were like sisters."

I was going to hear the story from Sara this time. I braced myself for the possibility that she would admit something about me, like what those girls admitted to Lisa last night.

"When she moved away, I felt empty inside. I had never felt that way before, and it was such an awful feeling. Like I was completely hollow and dark. I just wanted to fill it."

Lonely and empty was something I understood very well.

"Then you moved in and everyone kept saying, 'See? Here's your new friend!' and 'Isn't God good to bring you Clover?'

"I hated them for saying that. I hated every time you said 'hi' to me at the bus stop. I was in the room when Grandma was on the phone with your mom about Alpha Omega, and I hated her for inviting you. I didn't want you there, I wanted Bethany. I hated God for taking her away."

The emotion rose up from my gut like it did last night. Not because she was hurting my feelings, but because she was opening up to me.

"What changed?" I asked.

"You just kept trying!" Her eyes met mine. "You didn't stop trying."

Mrs. Belle's words rang in my ears …."Always assume people want to be your friend in due time."

"After my blood sugar attack, I was so afraid you would pull away from me. The next morning at the bus stop, Grandma Betsy wanted me to tell you how much you meant to me, but I was afraid I'd cry before school and ruin my makeup, so I didn't say anything."

So that's why Mrs. Belle was nudging her that morning.

"I was still so sad from losing Bethany, and I didn't want to lose you too. The thought of that made me feel sick."

The tears were hot in my eyes.

"Anyway, I DO have a point. I didn't want you, Clover, but you snuck up on me. I don't know why I decided to go on that walk with you, but I did. And I liked you. I was afraid of giving my heart away and getting hurt again. I was afraid of having a blood sugar attack and scaring you away."

It was clearly time to go get ready for school, but there was no way I could sit in a classroom and learn anything after that conversation.

"Getting to know Jesus can be the same way. He sneaks up on you and is surprisingly likeable. I just ... I don't know what else to say. But that ... he's cool. Jesus is cool."

I could tell she was finished. It was my turn. "What should I do?" I asked. "I don't know what to do."

"I don't know, Clover. Ask God. You seem to be the kind of girl who keeps trying. Do ... SOMETHING. Throw rocks. Try loving your enemies. Start somewhere." She got up to go in the house.

"I suck at throwing rocks," I reminded her. She laughed and went inside.

I took the dog back to Mrs. Belle's, and when I got home, I left a note for my mom on the table. *I am not feeling well. I'm going to go to bed. Please excuse me from school today and let me sleep.*

I couldn't wait to go back to bed and pull up the covers. There was a piece of paper on my nightstand, and I turned it over and saw the words I had written last night. I understood why those girls were pounding nails into the cross. I thought about The Challenge for this month, *Love Your Enemies*. I thought about how good it felt that Sara had opened up and told me the truth.

I got in bed and cried for a long time. It was the kind of cry that was happy, sad, angry, scared, confused, desperate, and thankful—all at the same time. I remembered what Sara had said, "Ask God. Do ... SOMETHING!!"

So I prayed. Really prayed. After crying for so long, I knew what I wanted. If God could give it to me, then I would know he was real.

"Dear God," I said. "I have made a decision. I will try to love my enemies. I will be nice to CSU and Robocop, but I want you to do something for me. I want to know why my mom wears a wig."

I wondered how much I could really ask for and, in the end, I decided to ask for the impossible. "And I want to go into her room. If you can do that for me, then we can talk again."

The Mission

I had propositioned God, and it would take time to figure out how to hold up my end of the deal and be nice to CSU and Robocop. Twinkle made a suggestion.

"You should start by calling them by their real names," she said. "That would be the beginning of love and respect, I think." Her voice was sarcastic, but her heart was serious. "And just because you made the commitment to be nice to them doesn't mean you have to try to be their best friend. Spend time watching them and try to find ways that you can be nice to them spontaneously."

That seemed fair. I knew CSU's name. She was in a lot of my classes. But Robocop was a hard one because, not only did I never see her, no one ever called her by her real name. I asked Twinkle what her name was, but she refused to tell. I thought it was mean that she was making me find out for myself. She called it tough love.

I hopped on Pinterest to try to find something I could make them as surprise Christmas gifts. Nothing jumped out at me, but there were a ton of Christmas ideas for my family and friends. It's impossible to find presents for girls that you don't know. Back to step one: Find out Robocop's name.

CSU was the key to that. She liked to talk, so I figured she would tell me. The trick would be to get to know her first. It would be rude to ask her about someone else before getting to know her. I sat by her in math class and, because we usually got our work done early, we had time to dork around.

"So, is there a story behind your name? Why did your mom name you Audrey?" Good starter question. If she talked about HER name first, then I could ask about Robocop.

She looked surprised that I had asked her a question. Everyone usually tried to avoid her.

"What? Oh yes, there IS a story!" she exclaimed with a gasp, like she was dying to share. "I was born with a baby tooth already in my mouth. That happens sometimes, but it's very rare. It wasn't a healthy tooth, so when my other teeth came in, it was all brown compared to the other ones. It fell out early."

I quickly realized that this story would have nothing to do with my question. Her stories were like a rabbit trail, and now I was stuck with her until the end of class.

"Then when I was one, I climbed to the top of a ten-speed bike and sat on it like I was riding it. Mom was really surprised that I could do that. She said that I must have rubber joints that could bend real far to get my legs up that high." CSU kept chattering without a point.

"Then when I was two, I walked by a tree and got stung five times by wasps and didn't even cry. Mom, however, was freaking out!" She pointed to the exact places that she was stung, like she was a four-year-old showing you her ouchies. Her face lit up and her voice was dramatic.

I was starting to be amused by her.

"Then when I was three, I had an epic nose bleed." She paused to see if I was listening.

So I responded, "Epic, huh?"

She nodded and used hand gestures, "It was GUSHING out. For five whole minutes. Mom called the ambulance, and they came out and did the same thing that she did, but having them there made her stop crying."

I remembered how I felt when Sara was having her diabetes attack and felt a little compassion for her mom, who must have been scared to see all that blood. "That must have been really scary for your mom," I said.

"It was!" she agreed. "Then when I was four, I got the flu and slept for two days straight. When my fever spiked to 105, Mom took me to the emergency room, and they did all kinds of stuff to me that I don't remember. I would wake up every now and then and see Mom and Dad looking at me all concerned. I do remember that."

She stopped talking for a moment, and I thought she was done.

"Soooo ... what does that have to do with your name?"

"Ack, my brain! I lost track of the point! Every year on my birthday, Mom tells me these stories and then says that it's her fault for naming me Audrey. Audrey means 'strength.' Mom thought that maybe the powers that be were trying to make me prove that I was strong." When she said "powers that be" she used a hand gesture that reminded me of my own mom.

"What about your name? Is there a story about your name?" Her words startled me.

"ME!?" I asked.

"Yeah you. What's your story?" she asked. No one said that I would have to share in this deal.

My name was different, and people asked me about it all the time. My parents, well ... my dad always said he made it up because he was lucky to have me. My mom never said anything about it and always moved on to other topics.

The bell rang and Audrey picked up her stuff and ran off like a happy gazelle. I watched her go and said out loud, "She is ... such an interesting breed, that girl!"

It was time for me to leave, too, but I didn't know which "me" was leaving. The "me" who wasn't sure if she would keep doing what everyone else did and make fun of her, or the "me" who was faintly interested in getting to know her.

I decided that the "me" who would leave the room would be the one who would stop calling her CSU and start calling her Audrey. It was a start.

Robocop, on the other hand, was impossible to get to know because she was like a scared little mouse that couldn't sit still for very long. Talking to her wasn't going to be easy. I watched her for a while, and it became clear that the only people she really talked to were the ones she confronted about the rules and their behavior. I might have to break the rules to get her attention.

I followed her for about four days and got to know her schedule. She always seemed to be the last person to get to class. And because I was following her, I was definitely the last one to my class, which meant the only seat left was by Audrey.

Audrey talked more and more about herself, and I found that I was captivated by her stories. She was fascinating. But sometimes I would yawn on purpose in case someone saw me listening to her. I didn't want the whole class to know I liked her.

After a couple days I said, "Hey Audrey, can I ask you something?"

"Sure," she said. Her life was an open book.

"I'm curious about a girl that I see around school." I was avoiding the name, Robocop. "I don't have any classes with her, but I see her barking orders at kids all the time. She really cares about the rules or something. Do you know who I'm talking about?"

"Yeah, I know her. I've been going to school with her since I was in kindergarten. What do you want to know?" She seemed ready to spill everything, but I just wanted to know her name.

"I want to know ..." I started, then paused to think if I should be more subtle. "I want to know her name." I decided to be blunt. My brain was plumb out of creativity.

"Oh. Her name is Nat." That's all she said. No other details.

"Okay. Thanks," I said.

Audrey looked at me to make sure that was all I wanted. She didn't offer anything extra like she usually did.

We stared at each other.

"So. Okay, then." I turned forward in my seat. It was my first awkward silent moment with Audrey. I would definitely have to tell Twinkle that it was possible. I would also tell her that my mission was accomplished, and I had both names now.

I wondered how it worked to have a deal with God. Do I tell him about my baby steps, and then keep going with the kindness? Do I just wait for his turn now to reveal the things I asked about, the wig and the room?

Later that night, I decided to tell God about the names, just in case he had missed the effort.

I looked up at my ceiling and said, "Nat and Audrey, God. Their names are Nat and Audrey. Your turn."

I put my hand up and did an air high five to tag God like they do in pro wrestling.

Christmas Break

$\mathcal{B}$y now, I had made around $200 walking the dog, and I celebrated alone in my troll doll haven. I had never seen so much money.

One more day of school, then we were off for a couple weeks for Christmas. When I came home from walking the dog, I saw a large envelope on the porch that said:

More pictures for your scrapbook
from your Secret Santa!

Whoever it was knew my schedule and knew that I would be out walking the dog. I hated that I would never know who gave me these gifts.

Inside were more pictures for my scrapbook. This time the pictures seemed to be really focused on the deeper things of life. There were pictures from school of me following Nat around to figure out her schedule. There were pictures of Audrey and me together. There were even pictures of me with Sara, walking the dog down the street.

"Creepy!" I said out loud. If there hadn't been a note on the pictures that said they were from my Secret Santa, I might've thought I had a stalker. I decided to go back to Mrs. Belle's to show her the pictures, even though I'd be cutting it close for the bus. I'd go without a shower if I had to.

Before I even reached the doorstep, I saw my mom's shoes on the front step. Oh yeah, Tuesday was Bible study morning. I had forgotten.

I peeked in the window and saw Mrs. Belle, my mom, and Sara's mom, and there were three other women I didn't recognize. There was no way I was going to ask about the pictures now, so I went home and got ready for school.

I showed Sara and Twinkle the Secret Santa pictures on the bus, and they thought it was really cool and even said they wished they had a Secret Santa who was documenting their year. I still thought it was creepy, but they didn't seem to think so. I figured it was some Christian thing I didn't know about yet.

The last day before Christmas break finally arrived. We exploded off the bus after school, like kids escaping the torture chamber.

Sara and Twinkle came to my house, and my mom had made some treats to celebrate Christmas break. She filled plastic baggies with popcorn, then divided it down the middle and clamped it with a clothespin she'd decorated to look like a butterfly's body. The popcorn on each side of the clothespin looked like wings. Twinkle and Sara loved it, and I complained that it wasn't enough food.

I wanted to take about twenty popcorn butterflies to my room, but Twinkle started asking my mom personal questions and I couldn't believe she didn't change the subject.

"Where did you meet Mr. Mannerhouse?" Twinkle asked.

I had the sudden urge to change the subject to protect my mom. Whenever people asked her questions about the past, she usually said, "Oh that's boring stuff. You don't want to know." If she was pressed to answer, she'd get all flustered and leave the room. She never answered questions like these.

This time was different. She breathed in real deep like she was meditating on her choice to speak.

"Ah Twinkle, we were young. Tom and I were both interns at a company during our Juniah year of college. We had the same majah, so we worked in the same department."

What? My mom had never told me this before.

"Was it love at first sight?" Twinkle asked, a look of romance in her eye.

"Oh, right away!" my mom said. "He was smart and gorgeous and I was ...." She had reached some sort of sharing limit, and I could tell she was back to her usual flustered self. She quickly put on a sweet face and turned the attention to Twinkle.

"Why do you ask, Twinkle? Is there a boy in your life?"

Twinkle turned red. "Maybe!"

Sara and I gasped, "TWINKLE!!! WHO???" We slammed our hands down on the table and yelled, "Tell tell tell tell!!!"

Twinkle turned bright red, and my mom went to the freezer to grab some sugar-free ice cream bars. "I was going to put cotton candy in a waffle cone," Mom said, "to make faux ice cream cones, but I didn't want to kill Sara!"

"Thank you, Mrs. Mannerhouse," Sara chimed in. "I appreciate the love and affection."

I was just glad to have more food. I was so hungry.

"Okay, Twinkle, tell us everything," my mom said, happy to turn the attention away from her.

"His name is ...." She stopped. "You guys can't make fun of me if I tell you, and you CAN'T tell anyone that I like him." She looked at us to see if we agreed to the terms. "Promise me, you guys."

We put our right hands in the air, even my mom, and promised we wouldn't tell.

"His name is Kendrick, and I met him at another youth group that I went to with a family friend." She perked up at the sound of his name.

"And? So?" We used our girl powers to get more out of her.

"His name tag said K-Ricky, and I asked him about it. He sarcastically said his real name was Kendrick, but K-Ricky was a nickname he got in the war. I thought that was so random and funny, and I laughed pretty hard. Then I turned red and ignored him the rest of the night." Twinkle looked at us for affirmation.

"You didn't talk to him the rest of the night?" I asked. This proved that we were all doomed in the boy category.

"I was a kid once; that sounds about right!" my mom said. That was the second thing my mom dished out about her past. She was on a roll.

"Here take some popcorn to your room if you want. Go have fun!" She was done socializing, and for once, going to my room didn't seem as fun as staying around the table to see if my mom would talk more.

"Go on, girls, have fun!" She sent us off with a big bowl of popcorn that we could shovel into our mouths. We meandered back to my room.

I took out some craft supplies and put my friends to work. My brother had taken me shopping to buy a bunch of things that I found to make on Pinterest. He wouldn't do it unless I paid him $10. So typical.

We filled clear ornaments with different colors of Jelly Bellies and wrote a different name for God in permanent marker on the outside of each one.

"This is so cool," Twinkle said, "where'd you get this idea?"

"On the internet of course. I looked up Christian gift ideas and found a ton of them. The only reason I know these are different names for God is because that's what the caption of the project said. I thought his first name was Jesus and his last name was Christ."

Sara and Twinkle chuckled and remembered when they had thought that too.

When we were finished, I pulled out a couple presents for them.

"Here guys. I can't wait until Christmas. I want you to open them now."

I handed each of them a small box wrapped in brown paper. I had drawn a picture of Jesus in a superhero cape on Sara's. The caption said, "More than meets the eye. Robots in disguise!" It was a song reference to a kid's toy. The kid's toy had a double meaning. I hoped she got what I meant after our life-changing talk on her front porch.

"Do you get it, Sara? Do you know the toy with that song?" I asked.

She sang, "Robots in disguise!" and then exclaimed, "TRANS-FORMERS!" and then she thought about Jesus in a cape singing the song. "Ah yes. Jesus IS a transformer. I get it!"

Twinkle smiled. "Their names are Audrey and Nat. You've transformed already, Clover."

"Okay, okay shhhhh. I'm not ready to have the Jesus talk yet. I'm just trying out some things." I gave Twinkle her present to change the subject.

I had drawn a bright star above a nativity scene on one side of her box. On the other side, I drew a bright star above a woman who was giving birth outside in a tub of water in Colorado. Twinkle had told me the story about her birth when I first met her at Alpha Omega. Her parents had named her after the stars that shone as her mom gave birth to her outside.

"Oh my GOSH, Clover … this is so gross and so appropriate all at the same time! It makes me think about the fact that the same stars were shining when Jesus was born as the night I was born!!! I was named after the stars that were shining down on baby Jesus. HOW COOL IS THAT?"

"Okay, okay, open them!!" I said, excited to surprise my friends.

They ripped open their presents. Inside were white T-shirts that I had tie-dyed with a sharpie. I was so excited when I found out how to make them on YouTube.

"How did you do this?" Sara asked.

"It's really easy," I said. "You take a sharpie and draw pin point dots or circles anywhere you want on the shirt. Then you spray rubbing alcohol on the ink, and it bleeds out randomly to make these cool designs." I had done Sara's in black pin dot flowers all on the left side, and Twinkle's was the same style but done in red. "I made a green one for myself, so we could all have one." It was like we had our own little club.

"You MADE these?" Twinkle asked.

"Yeah, you haven't seen them? They are huge in Los Angeles. Do you like them?" I was glad they were so excited.

"Totally! You have to teach us how to do it. I'm putting mine on," said Twinkle. Sara put hers on too, but she went to the bathroom to change. Modest girl.

I called my mom in to take our picture. I didn't think it would be a Secret Santa foul to add my own photos to *My Journey* scrapbook. The first note said I could.

The next couple days went by fast. I put the ornaments filled with Jelly Bellies on Mrs. Belle's front step. Hopefully she would not mind getting only one present from her Secret Santa.

On Christmas Eve, I psyched myself up to receive the stupid ornament from my mom. As it turned out, she had a couple surprises up her sleeve. She cooked a nice dinner for us, which she was capable of doing but rarely did. Then we had to go around the table and tell each person why we were proud of them, and I shared how I was proud of my mom because she told my friends and me how she and my dad met.

We were going to our first Christmas Eve church service after dinner, and my mom went to her room to get ready. When she came out of the bedroom, she was wearing a very conservative and normal looking wig. Nothing gaudy or fake looking. My dad and I were sitting on the couch, and he whistled at her and I clapped. She looked semi-normal.

After church, we came home to open our Christmas Eve presents, but this time, I wanted to give my mom her present before she could give me mine.

"You and Dad will have to open that toogethah!" I said with my pointer fingers.

They sat snug on the couch and opened their gift. My mom did a Maggie Ann Mannerhouse squeal when she opened their ornament. It was a Barbie and Ken doll that were superglued together, arm in arm. Barbie had a sash that said, "Maggie Ann" and the Ken's sash said "Tom."

She got up and put the ornament on a sturdy branch. It was a heavy ornament, but not the most gaudy one we had, unfortunately. She grabbed a familiar-sized package, and before she handed it to me, she said, "This will be the last boy ornament you will get, Clovah."

"Really? Gosh, I don't know if I'm ready for that. This better be a good finale!" I felt kind of sad to leave the tradition behind.

When I saw her creation it was, indeed, the best one yet, although I wouldn't have thought that three months ago. It was a store-bought manger scene small enough to fit in both my hands. My mom had glued a picture of my face on one of the shepherds, like I was a participant on that night. I had a silly grin in my picture. It was perfect. Jesus was my final boy. My mom put it on the tree for me, just like old times.

When we were done with presents it was late, but my dad and I snuggled on the couch for a while. I hoped that I never got too old to snuggle with him. After a bit he asked me, "What are you thinking about, Clover?" I got up and started off to my bedroom and said, "Transformers."

He yelled to me as I walked into my room, "You aren't getting one for Christmas you know!!!"

He was wrong. My mom had just put one on the tree.

Finding Treasure

*G*oing back to school, I suppose, was inevitable. They always make you go back.

Lisa had thrown a great New Year's Eve party at Mrs. Belle's house, and I was starting to look forward to going back to Alpha Omega. Three weeks was long enough to make me miss it, and I realized that now I was going because I wanted to, for me.

Twinkle, Sara, and I had planned to wear our Sharpie tie-dyed shirts on the first day of school. They were a big hit. All the girls wanted them. Even some boys were digging it.

On the bus after school, we made a plan. We would take T-shirt orders during the week and get together every Friday night to make them. They could dry over the weekend and be delivered on Monday.

We split the money three ways. Twinkle was the fierce salesman, I had the cash to get the supplies up front, and Sara was the master artist. We were equal partners.

The very first Alpha Omega meeting of the year was parents' night. I didn't expect to bring my parents, but no one told

THEM that. They both came and stayed for the evening. I was bummed.

We walked in the door, and Lisa was one of the greeters. Her hair was starting to grow back which was a huge deal. I bet she was thrilled to have hope for a full head of hair one day.

The last time my mom was in the same room with Lisa, it didn't go well, but this time my mom acted like she always hung around semi-bald people, and it didn't even phase her. What was going on with her? She had shared about her past a tiny bit before Christmas, she had given me the last boy ornament ever, there was a conservative wig on her head, and now she wasn't afraid of Lisa's bald head?

They hugged, and my mom whispered in Lisa's ear, like they knew each other.

Lisa hugged me, too, and I whispered in her ear just like my mom did, "Does my mom know you?"

She pulled back and smiled, "That's her story to tell."

Great. I would never know.

We found Twinkle and her mom and sat by them. Sara was sitting up front with her mom and Mrs. Belle. I felt a little sad that my favorite girl wasn't sitting by me, but I understood. It was family night.

Mrs. Belle was the speaker as usual. "Welcome friends and parents. For those of you who have been coming to Alpha Omega for a couple years now, you know that the first meeting in January is always parents' night.

Our theme this year has been Treasure. I want to ask you, and please don't embarrass me: what is kingdom treasure?"

We all answered dutifully, "People." I heard my parents' voices booming out over mine enthusiastically, "PEOPLE!" I looked over at them.

Mrs. Belle said, "Surprise! Your parents have been studying the same thing in their own Bible studies. They are also students. They have been receiving the same challenges that you have."

I looked over at my mom. I knew she was going over to Mrs. Belle's every Tuesday morning, but I didn't think anything of it. Maybe that was the source of her recent changes. She had given me the very last ornament and had chosen Jesus to be my last boy. I assumed that she gave it to me out of ignorance. Maybe it went deeper. Maybe she knew something too.

Mrs. Belle went on. "Tonight, we will focus on Jesus as the treasure instead of people."

She read from Matthew 13 but first said, "In verse 44, there is a guy that stumbles upon treasure." She read, "*The Kingdom of Heaven is like treasure hidden in a field, which a man found and covered up. Then in his joy he goes and sells all that he has and buys that field.*"

She looked up from the Bible and again said, "In verse 45, there is a man that searches for a long time." Then she read, "*Again, the kingdom of heaven is like a merchant in search of fine pearls, who, on finding one pearl of great value, went and sold all that he had and bought it.*"

She stepped down and went to sit by Sara and her mom. The lights went dim and a screen came up out of the wall. A video started playing. The title showed up on the screen first:

The ninth graders find treasure: Stumbling upon Jesus

The video showed a group of ninth grade girls getting ready for an outing. They were in the bathroom curling their hair and putting on their makeup. It reminded me of my birthday party when Sara and Twinkle and I sat on my bed and played around with makeup together.

The girls were dropped off at the mall, and they walked into a store to look for clothes. They came in and out of changing rooms, wearing new outfits and laughing. It reminded me of a music video.

They walked down the mall with a bunch of bags full of clothes that only worldly rich girls would be able to buy.

Suddenly the music changed and the girls saw Lisa sitting at a table in a coffee shop. I hadn't seen it coming. These were the same girls that had confessed what they had done to Lisa during Alpha Omega. This was a reenactment of that moment, and this time I was forced to watch it with my parents. I wondered if my mom would leave.

I watched the girls run up and steal her hat. It was all there. The stealing and the hiding. The close up of Lisa's face was real. Her emotion and struggle showed through on her face. She stood up and spent all her money to buy them coffee and, when she did that, a man came out of nowhere and joined her. He had a beard and was carrying a Bible, so I knew it must be Jesus. When Lisa gave them the coffee, Jesus shook their hands and hugged them.

The screen went black and we saw these words:

**When Lisa bought us coffee, we stumbled upon Jesus.
She gave us mercy when we didn't deserve it.
That surprised us. Jesus surprised us.**

The screen went black again and there were more words:

Ninth grader finds treasure: Searching for a long time

Next we saw a slide show of a bunch of still pictures that centered around one girl that I didn't recognize. She seemed lively and was always surrounded by a bunch of friends.

The pictures showed the girl at various Alpha Omega meetings. One picture caught my attention. She was standing next to Mrs. Belle and was holding a check for $1,000. I wondered how long Mrs. Belle had been doing The Challenge. This was obviously taken at least two years ago because I knew Lisa had gotten it last year.

Then the pictures changed again. Now they didn't center around the girl, but around a hospital. I saw that same girl sitting in a chair, surrounded by Mrs. Belle and family. There was a bag with a tube going into her arm. The tube was full of a yellow-orange color, and it looked like toxic waste. The people in the picture held up a sign to document the occasion: *First chemo treatment. You can beat it, Lisa!!! We love you!*

How in the world could that be Lisa? It didn't look anything like her. I had never seen her with a round face and a full head of hair. It had never occurred to me that Lisa looked different before she was sick.

The next series of pictures were about her treatment and recovery and her Bible study groups. At the end, there was a picture of Lisa getting dunked under water with a bunch of folks surrounding her.

The screen went black and the words on the screen were Lisa's:

I had to search for Jesus for a long time.
Thanks to Mrs. Belle and my friends at Alpha Omega,
I was introduced to Jesus and a new way of life.

The lights came back on and my mom was still in the room! I couldn't believe it.

Mrs. Belle came back up to speak. "Being on a search for Jesus is a lot like being on a search for the man you will marry. Some of you will find him accidentally, and some of you will search and search."

I saw my dad grab my mom's hand.

"I had no idea what I was looking for when I found Mr. Belle. I went to university and my goal was to become a teacher, but I also wanted to get my M.R.S. degree. I was on a search for a husband, after all, and college had lots of smart and capable young men!" Mrs. Belle giggled like she was young again.

"To pay for college, I got a job at Sears, and Mr. Belle was one of the managers there. He was young and fresh out of college, and he had GOALS!!

"We often ate lunch together, and I was mesmerized by him. He would talk about simple things, and I adored his voice.

"Perhaps what sold me completely was the day we took a stroll through the store on our break. He walked me through the new television section, and that was when televisions were just becoming popular.

"He said, 'Betsy do you see this television? Someday I am going to sell the things you see in this store on this television. It will be a show that is a store. You will be able to buy anything you want from your own home!'

"That's when I knew I wanted Mr. Belle. It wasn't like I knew everything about him, my goodness no. Every time I was with him, I learned more things. I still wanted him to be my one and only.

"Jesus is a lot like that. Whether you stumble upon him or search forever, entering into a relationship with Jesus is a lot like saying 'yes' to the man you will marry. You know his worth and value, and you choose him. You don't understand everything about him, and you have a lot to learn, but you choose him."

Mrs. Belle nodded to the back and, like always, the ninth graders came up front to help. They were holding something, but I couldn't see what it was.

Sara and her mom got up. Sara was carrying the guitar. I looked at Twinkle and felt proud that I had given it to her.

"Do you think she is going to play a song?" I whispered.

"I don't know." She was as curious as I was.

Mrs. Belle said, "Each of these helpers has a ring. They aren't meant to fit your finger literally, but it's meant to be a symbol of your 'yes.' If you've never said 'yes' to Jesus before and you want to tonight, then come up and get a ring when you are ready. There will be some music as you think about it."

Sara started playing an easy but hauntingly beautiful song that she had written.

> If I wanted safety, I would walk away.
> If I wanted comfort, I wouldn't choose you.
> There is something more,
> That my heart's dying for.
> The day you died for me.
>
> I want to go where you go.
> I want to die where you die.
> I want to live how you live.
> I want to be free.
>
> Today I say "yes" to your call
> Or I don't live at all.

As Sara played the song, she repeated some of the words for emphasis. Her voice rang out. It was clear and pure, luring us toward the invitation. I wanted to ask Twinkle if she knew that Sara could sing like that, but her eyes were closed and she'd lifted her hands up a bit. I didn't want to ruin her moment.

Both my mom and dad got up and walked forward to take a ring. I sat back and talked to Jesus, "If my mom walks up there and takes her wig off, then I'll go up and take a ring. We had a deal, God."

My mom and dad stood arm in arm while Mrs. Belle prayed for them. Other girls and their parents went forward too. Not a ton, but there were some. I sat and waited for God to hold up his end of the bargain. If Mrs. Belle's analogy rang true, then my treasure was going to have to work a little harder to woo me.

The Surprise

Things changed in our house after my parents took the rings. My mom cooked dinner and made us eat at the table instead of in front of the TV. We had to pray before we ate and tell what we were thankful for. My brother kept insisting that he was too old for thankfulness, but my parents made him do it anyway. He always said, "I'm thankful for my good skin."

My dad said he was thankful that the garbage man came once a week or that every day of the week ended in Y.

I would make up something and say that I was thankful that I had shoes or that we had food to eat. One time, just for fun, I said I was thankful for my brother, and he quickly said, "No you're not, Clover!" and my dad lifted his hand and said, "Hey, no fighting during thankful time!"

My mom often said she was thankful for her new relationship with Jesus. Then my brother would roll his eyes, and my dad would say, "Amen, Maggie Ann!"

In a nutshell, my parents were trying to change our family culture, and my brother and I weren't going to give up without a fight.

At least I knew what to expect at school. Same teachers, same routine, same kids in my classes. The one thing different was that I was now calling CSU and Robocop Audrey and Nat to their faces AND behind their back. Somehow calling them by their real names made them seem like real people.

The change might have stopped right there, except for an unexpected conversation with Nat before lunch one day.

She came up to me and demanded, "You are going to sit with Audrey and me during lunch today. We want to place an order."

I couldn't hide my surprise that she was interested in joining the school epidemic of wearing our tie-dyed shirts. "Sure, I'll see if Sara and Twinkle want to come too."

"We want shirts like yours," Audrey said.

"Okay," said Twinkle. She got out her notebook where she kept all the orders, "What kind of colors and styles do you like?"

"We want shirts like yours," Audrey said again.

"You mean you want the same style and colors as ours?" Twinkle asked. We had made a serious effort to make every order different from ours. People could draw a design they liked on paper and we would transfer it to the shirt, but no one could have our design. That was just for us.

Twinkle looked at Sara, then back at me. I spoke up first because I figured that since I had made the commitment to be nice to them, I should be the one to break the hard news gently.

"I'm sorry, but our design is sort of something just for us. Sort of like a company logo, you know? We don't make this design for others. It's not for sale. Would you like a different design?" I was trying to be as nice as possible, yet firm.

It was Audrey's turn to plead her case, "I want to be part of your group, Clover. I like sitting with you in class. I like being your friend."

I had to admit that melted my heart all the way down to my toes.

Nat pleaded her case in a very Robocop sort of way, and I held my tongue, "It's not like I don't look on the internet, you know. It's not against the law for anyone to replicate them. I can figure out how to make one just like yours if you won't make it for me."

Audrey was the diplomatic one. "Hey Nat, would you mind going to get me some milk?" She handed her a dollar. "I would really love some help getting my milk."

Nat grabbed her dollar and said, "Sure!" and ran off like a little Golden Retriever ready to serve her master.

Audrey leaned in. "Please consider making us the shirts. It would mean so much to Nat. She can't speak with a soft heart, and she gets that from her dad. He's a military officer, and I've been to her house. He isn't kind. I can't say anything more because she is coming back. Google her dad, Arthur French, and you'll see what I mean." Audrey quickly changed the subject. "So you have our order then? Great. What color do you want, Nat?"

"I want mine to look like Sara's," Nat said. Sara shifted in her seat.

Audrey filled the rest of the lunch hour with stories about her life, and she was less charming and winsome than ever. Probably because she had jimmied her way into my business.

That afternoon, we debriefed the lunch conversation on the bus.

"We need to talk about that lunch order. My guess is that you both want to do it?" I questioned. I was openly assuming they would take the Christian high road.

Twinkle jumped in, "Oh, my gosh, no! It took everything in me to be nice and listen to them instead of blow them off. Especially after what Nat said about making her own. That was really rude."

Sara was the compassionate one, "But you heard Audrey. It's not about the shirts. She wants friends. We could make her a shirt that looks like ours, but what she really wants is to belong. You both moved here this year; you should totally get that."

"Yeah, that sort of melted my heart a little bit, but then Nat unmelted it," I admitted.

"I think Nat needs a friend too, and I wonder if Audrey has been reaching out to her. Let's not decide until we Google Nat's dad. Maybe we should do that Friday night? We'll have enough supplies if we decide to do it. Let's be perfect!" Sara had a way of inspiring us.

"Somebody remember the name Arthur French so we can Google him. Friday is a long way off, and I don't want us to forget!" I said.

On Friday night we got together at Twinkle's house to fill our orders and look up Arthur French. We had ten shirts to make, or twelve if the Google search went as Audrey hoped.

We looked up "Arthur French, Hitlery, California," and a couple articles appeared with some pictures of Nat.

"Click on that one," Twinkle said.

I clicked on the article and read it aloud.

Local Man Deemed Most Disciplined Man Alive

According to the Guinness Book of World Records, our very own Arthur French is the most disciplined man alive.

Last June, Arthur submitted a schedule to the World Record officials that he adopted while he was in boot camp when he was 19 years old. He sent 9,125 pages of his journal that documented his daily activities for the past 25 years.

On each page were 45 regimented activities that he completed by 22:00 each day.

He got up at the same time every day and ran 5 miles at the same speed. He ate the same breakfast, lunch, and dinner. He brushed his teeth with 10 circles for each area of his mouth 3 times a day. He read one chapter of a book, wrote one letter, called a friend, and made his bed, to name a few things.

Arthur and his wife met in the military and she finds his discipline predictable. "I know what to expect every day. Part of his discipline is helping out around the house, and what wife doesn't like that?"

There was more to the article, but we didn't read it.

"No wonder Nat is a drill sergeant! Can you imagine living with someone that strict? Forty-five things that have to be done daily?" I said, connecting some dots.

"Yeah, what if Nat got sick and had to go to the hospital? Would he break his routine to take her?" Twinkle asked.

"What do you think his wedding day was like with all those disciplines?" I made a face signifying that I would not have married him.

"Do you remember that Audrey said she'd been to their house, and he's mean? If Nat has lived a life where discipline comes first, even before her, no wonder she reacted badly when we wouldn't make her a shirt. She is dying for someone to break the rules for her, you know?" Sara was so wise.

"Poor thing!!" Twinkle and I agreed that Nat needed that kind of attention.

"You never know what is underneath, do you?" I said out loud. "I've had such a hard time with Mrs. Belle and her talks about people being treasure and how we need to love hard people. But the more I've gotten to know Audrey and Nat and the more I've heard their stories, I sort of want to love them. That's not normal for me."

We didn't need to talk about it anymore—it was a given that we would make the shirts. No question.

Twinkle and Sara got out the white T-shirts and put flat cereal boxes inside them, so the ink wouldn't bleed through. I was still messing around on the computer and asked, "Hey, have you guys ever Googled yourselves? I wonder what's on here about me?"

"Oh yeah," Twinkle said. "I did it last year, and I'm pretty boring. It only brought up my Instagram account. I Googled my dad and that was much more exciting ...." Twinkle stopped talking and looked up to see the horror on my face. "Clover! What are you reading? What did you find?"

I couldn't talk, and I couldn't breathe. I wasn't sure I even wanted to keep reading.

I had put my name in the search engine, and evidently there were many articles about my family and me from very early in my life. I scrolled down until I reached one that mentioned both my parents' names. It wasn't an article I was emotionally ready to read. The headline said:

Woman and Unborn Child Saved in Car Accident

Maggie Ann Mannerhouse

The article and others like it explained that my mom had been in a terrible car accident when she was eight months pregnant with me. It was her last day of work before she took maternity leave. She picked up my brother from daycare and ran a red light on her way home. Her car was T-boned on the driver's side.

My brother was fine, but my mom was airlifted to the hospital. The wing mirror on the outside of the car flew through the window, broke her jaw, ripped off her ear and almost all of the left side of her scalp. She also had a broken leg and hip.

The impact was serious enough to cause my life-giving placenta to tear. I was in danger of not getting enough oxygen, and my mom was in danger of bleeding to death, in addition to her face and head being badly injured. The articles said we were both lucky to be alive.

My mom had a blood transfusion and several surgeries to wire her jaw shut and reconstruct her ear, head, and face. They actually found the remains of her ear lying on the seat next to my brother, and the paramedics quickly put it on ice to try to save it. I stayed in the NICU for about two weeks and left the hospital without any permanent damage.

"Are you okay?" Twinkle asked me. "I'm so sorry."

"Why don't I know about this?" I asked. I was still in shock.

"What about your baby pictures? You have pictures of your mom and you together when you were born, right?" Twinkle was sure there were clues.

"Sure, I have pictures of myself back then." I was trying to think if I had ever seen a picture of my mom holding me in the hospital or if we had any family pictures from when I was a baby. It couldn't be possible that I had never seen pictures of me with my family when I was a baby, could it?

"Can I print this article on your printer?" I asked Twinkle. "I want to take it to Mrs. Belle." I hit print and read more about the beginning of my life that had been kept a secret.

"I don't feel like making T-shirts," I said. "Would it be okay if I left and let you guys finish?" They practically pushed me out the door.

Instead of going home, I headed straight to Mrs. Belle's house. I didn't know if she would be home on a Friday night, but I had to process what I'd just learned with an adult that I trusted. I rang the doorbell and was surprised that Lisa answered it, her frizzy hair stumps sticking out all over. There seemed to be some sort of self-image support group going on. Behind Lisa there were several bald women and one woman with short hair on one side and a bald head on the other.

I didn't recognize her at first. She wasn't wearing makeup or her high heels. Even though I had read that my mom had lost part of her scalp, there was no way that woman in front of me was Maggie Ann Mannerhouse.

"I'm sorry, I didn't know you were having a party," I said to the silence. They all stared at me, not knowing how to confront the issue at hand.

"Clovah?" I heard from the woman who was definitely not my mom.

I walked forward to the stranger, staring at her the whole way. She certainly sounded like my mother.

I clutched the article in my hands like a security blanket. When she came close, I handed it to her. "So is this true?" She looked at it and nodded in affirmation.

"I haven't been strong enough to tell you, Clovah. I've had so much shame about it that I was afraid to tell you. I died inside that day. I only wish I could've told you before you found out on your own. I'm so sorry, Clovah," she spewed out.

My mom started to cry as she squeezed out the words, "I was so afraid you would hate me like I've hated myself." This was the first time I got to see her emotion before the bathtub did.

Without saying anything, I turned around and left. I didn't even close the door behind me. My dad met me at the house. My mom had obviously called or texted to let him know something happened.

I fell into his arms and cried. My dad sat me down on the couch, and I sobbed for the woman at Mrs. Belle's house that I didn't know. That I wasn't sure I wanted to know. She had kept things from me. She had shut me out. Did she think I was just going to run into her arms and accept the truth? Did she think I would buy her coffee, like Lisa did with the girls who stole her hat?

Who was this mom that didn't wear makeup and let the world see her half bald head? Who was this mom that cried in front of me? Who was this mom that went to a support group to share her deep feelings and face them? I didn't know her.

My dad listened and stroked my shoulder. When I finished crying, he asked if I wanted to know the whole story.

"Yeah. But I want to hear it from you," I said.

He kissed the top of my head. "I met your mom while we were interns at a huge company that sold competitive products for athletic gear. It was a start-up company that hired cheap college interns to do marketing.

"The day they introduced us, I saw your mom and was determined to get to know her. She was beautiful and gentle and lovely. Turns out she was also smart and creative. Do you know who our supervisor was the most impressed with on our marketing team?" His set up was obvious.

"Mom?" I squeaked out.

"Yep. Your mom." He paused to remember those days. He spoke slowly and thoughtfully, like a grandfather talking about the olden days.

"We both got hired on full time after college. She was the head of Marketing, and I was under her as her employee. She was brilliant, Clover. She would take the younger interns and develop them and use their promising ideas. And then she put the rest of us to work to implement those ideas and make them happen.

"It was her idea to hire interns who weren't marketing majors, but people in the real world who understood the internet. She helped us market through the internet when that was cutting edge." I could tell my dad was really impressed with her.

This woman he spoke of was so different than the Maggie Ann Mannerhouse that I knew. "But she never touches the computer now. It's like she doesn't know how to use it," I said.

"Yep. She used to do a lot of things that she doesn't do anymore. She had fire behind her eyes and a kick in her step. The day of the accident changed her life. It changed both our lives.

"I was still at work writing up an ad when I got the call to go to the hospital. I could tell it was serious, and I thought that I was going to lose you, Clover, and my wife too. I waited in the emergency room for hours and hours. I paced the floor over and over again. Do you know how many tiles there are in the ER waiting room?"

"How many?"

"One thousand thirty-four tiles. I counted them over and over to get my mind off of the terrible thought that I would never see my sweet Mammy again."

"Mammy?"

"I called her Mammy before the accident. It's her initials Maggie Ann Mannerhouse with an M.Y., Mammy."

"That's cute, Dad."

"The doctor came out and told me that he saved both my baby girl and my wife, but we would have to wait a couple days to see if you had any brain damage from the lack of oxygen. Then he asked if I wanted to see you.

"We didn't know if you were going to be a boy or girl. We had known with your brother, but this time we wanted it to be a surprise. Finding out you were a girl after a tragic car accident was not the experience I had pictured, but I was so thrilled.

"You had an oxygen tube in your nose and monitors taped on your skin. You looked so tiny and lonely in the NICU, and I cried and cried. I got to hold you and sing to you. I kept saying that we were lucky to have you alive. You were our four-leaf Clover. Clover was your nickname initially, and it stuck."

"If it's a nickname, does that mean that I have another real name?" I asked.

"Yes, but I think your mother should tell you. That's too personal for me to share alone," he said.

"I finally got to see your mom, and that was hard. Her mouth was wired shut and her head was bandaged. She didn't look like the Maggie Ann that I knew. Her face was huge and puffy. Her eyes were swollen shut.

"When she finally woke up, I had to get to know the woman that was now my wife. She was horrified of so many things. She was horrified that she ran the red light that could've killed her baby and our son. She was horrified that her body might reject her sewn on ear and that her scalp wouldn't grow hair on the left side of her head. She was horrified that her face looked so different from the jaw surgery and nerve damage.

"I didn't know how scarred she was until we got home and started to live our life.

"She wouldn't talk about the accident, wouldn't let anyone take any pictures of the two of you together until you were about two years old because it reminded her of the trauma, which she never wanted to relive or think about again. She never went back to work. She was terrified that people would ask her about it. She didn't let me call her Mammy. She stuffed it. She stuffed it all inside."

"So you never talked about it … ever?" I asked.

"She doesn't have to talk for me to know what's inside, Clover. I look at you every day and can't imagine what it would feel like to know that I could've killed or disabled you. She lives with that guilt every day."

"But, nothing happened to me, Dad." I wondered if there was something I didn't understand. There didn't seem to be any problem from my point of view. I lived. I am fine.

"Oh sweetie, the 'terrible parent' fairy can come and sit on your shoulder and whisper insults in your ear when things *almost* happen, just as much as when things actually *do* happen.

"I did fall in love with the new Maggie Ann. Even though she stuffed the pain, she never stuffed me. She clung closer to me, and that really helped. She needed me to love her through it, and I did.

"There were times when I didn't know if I could make it another day. We had a ton of medical bills, and it nearly broke us. We endured a huge depression spell when she realized that even after speech therapy, she would never talk the same. Every time she opened her mouth, she was reminded of the accident. She refused to talk for about a week, and I could barely stand it. I eventually quit my job because it was too painful for her to hear about her old life through me. The only thing that kept her from going back to the old Maggie was herself, her unwillingness to face her past. I accepted that. I didn't know what else I could do.

"Luckily, with my marketing experience, I was able to do commercials and lawyer ads. You probably remember how much we had to weigh and measure our money. It wasn't a great life for you kids.

"I do love it here, Clover, and a lot has changed for the good. Your mom has friends, and she is opening up and dealing with things. I'm not getting my old Maggie Ann back; I'm getting a new Maggie Ann. The night she went up and took the ring, she forgave herself for running the red light. She's been lighter and happier. She wears a normal wig now, like she doesn't have to prove something or make up for something she lost."

The door opened and my mom walked in. She was quiet and careful. She sat down and waited for me to open up to her.

My dad had let her hide herself all these years. Now that I knew the story, I wasn't going to be so gracious.

"I want to see your room," I said. It wasn't a question.

"I don't know if I'm ready for that, Clovah." She started to cry again. "It's my private place where I get to deal with things on my own terms. I don't know if I am ready to lose that control and let you see all of me just yet."

I walked down the hall huffing like the wolf in the three little pigs. I yelled and slammed my hand on the door, "It's not about you tonight, Mom!" I slammed my hands harder. "Maybe I'M ready! Maybe I want you to let me in. Maybe I need to feel like a kid with a normal mom who wants me in her bedroom. Maybe I need to feel … like you want me." I leaned against her door and slid to the floor, sobbing.

I heard the key slip in the lock, and when I looked up, both Mom and Dad extended their hands to lift me up.

I didn't see anything special inside at first. There was a bed and two dressers and a place for shoes. Maybe I expected more secrets to be revealed? On one wall was a shelf full of her wigs. They were neatly brushed.

On the wall adjacent to her bed was, at first glance, a pretty collage. But the more I looked at it, I realized it was actually a self-punishment mural. Pinned up on a large piece of corkboard were pictures of beautiful women and their babies. Young moms happily pulling their kids in wagons. Beauty secret articles and *Seventeen* magazine articles, "Fifty ways to a better YOU!" In the center was a picture of Maggie Ann Mannerhouse in the hospital after the accident and articles from the newspaper that I had found on Google, stuck with pins.

We sat on the bed and stared at the collage of self-hatred. "Every time your mom felt like a terrible mother," Dad said, "she came in here and added a pin to her picture and articles. She blamed everything on that accident."

My mom opened up. "Ever since the accident, I've felt like everything was my fault. Mrs. Belle said I have been seeing life through guilt glasses. If you got sick, Clovah, it was my fault because I couldn't nurse you as a baby. If you didn't get along with your brother, it was my fault because maybe I didn't hold you enough those first four months while I was recuperating. If you didn't get along with kids at school, then maybe it was my fault because we didn't have money to sign you up for a soccer team or the fun camps. I kept trying hardah and hardah to be the prettiest mom and be bettah so that you would have a normal life like all the other kids. If we nevah had that accident, life would've been perfect ...."

"Like those pictures of those moms on the wall?" I made the connection.

"Yes. I was obsessed with magazines of moms who had a perfect life because I wanted to make myself into that," she affirmed.

"So why did you freak out when you caught me in here before we moved in? There was nothing here yet," I asked.

"Clovah, this room and the bathroom is the only place that I can control. The only place where I know I can deal with life on my own terms. When I saw you in the bathroom I freaked out, sort of like an anorexic would freak if you made her eat a plate of food. This room is my place, my room," she explained.

She went into the bathroom and opened a closet. She pulled out a picture of herself with Dad and my brother, her belly full and round. "This picture was taken a month before the accident."

Dad was right. She was beautiful. Her face was pure and silky. Her hair was long and gorgeous, just like her wigs, but it was real.

"Can I see what it's like now?" I asked, and Mom let me touch her head and her ear. I could see where they had stitched it back on, and I compared her new face with the one in the picture. Her smile was different because of the nerve damage. She showed me where she couldn't feel her face if I touched it.

"I think you are just as beautiful now, Mom," I said.

"Clovah." She was crying pretty hard now, and it made me uneasy. Moms are supposed to be okay, so they can care for you. I wondered who was going to make everything okay for Mom. Dad put his arm around her.

"Mrs. Belle told me that I wouldn't be totally free until I asked you to forgive me," she said. "I'm so sorry I ran that red light. I am sorry that I didn't give you the kind of life you were meant to live. I am so sorry ..." she was sobbing, "... that I almost killed you." I started crying too. I held onto her and didn't want to let her go.

"It's okay, Mom. You didn't mean to. I don't feel bad about our life." We both had snot running out of our noses, and Dad ran to get some toilet paper, so we could regain a little dignity. We looked at each other and laughed and hugged because we were such a mess, and it was oddly funny and beautiful and messy and ... wonderful.

"Dad said that Clover is my nickname. What's my real name?" I asked.

"Oh. You told her about that, Tom?" It seemed to be another layer of hurt.

"I think it's time she knew, Maggie Ann," he said.

She looked at me and stroked my face with her hand. It was good to feel that warmth from her. "When I was lying in the hospital unable to contribute, your dad named you Margaret Ann Mannerhouse ... after me. I was mad because I hated myself. You deserved a bettah name."

What? My name was Margaret Ann Mannerhouse, just like Mom. I would have to let that sink in.

"I like it, Mom. Just don't tell Ryan. He'll start calling me Margie just to get my goat," I said. Although, in secret, I really liked the name Margie. I thought it was cute.

That meaningful moment might have continued, but Ryan came home.

He took one look in the room and said, "Woah! Looks like you guys are having a snot fest. I will not be joining you!" He turned to go to his room, but saw Mom's head. "What happened to your face, Mom?" We busted out laughing. It was quite possible that he never noticed that Mom ever wore a wig ... boys!

"Come on in, son," Dad said. "We need to have a little talk."

I went to my room to let them have their moment that, consequently, took one-tenth of the time that it did with me.

The whole story played out in my mind as I fell asleep. What started out as a traumatic surprise ended up as a peaceful resolution to the mystery I had longed to solve. Mom opened her door for me, the door of her heart.

Now to go through another door.

The Ring

I went to Mrs. Belle's house in the morning, not to walk the dog, but to talk to her. It was a Saturday morning, but I remembered she had said that she always got up at 6:30, even on weekends. I was tired, but there was something I needed to do, and I wanted to get it done. I had made a bargain with God and, after last night, there was nothing to hold me back from finishing the deal.

Not only was Mrs. Belle up, she was outside on the bench, throwing a ball to the dog.

"Well, hello," she said. "I wondered if I might see you this morning. Big night last night for you and your family."

I sat next to her, rubbed my eyes, and nodded. "I'm tired. It's a good tired though," I said.

"I bet you are," she empathized.

"Funny thing is that I've been wanting this. I've always felt like there was something Mom was hiding, and I wanted to know what it was ...."

Mrs. Belle interrupted me. "But when it finally happened, you didn't really want to know?" she asked.

"YES!" I exclaimed. She hit the nail right on the head.

"We get used to our life don't we?" She threw the ball to the dog, and he ran after it like his life depended on it.

"You know," she said, "Jesus said we should take the narrow road, through him. He said that it was a tough road and that not many people would take it. To be able to follow Jesus, we have to face some real things, and I understand why people don't want to do it. It's hard."

"It was just an accident, Mrs. Belle. Nobody died. I don't understand why this was so hard for Mom," I said.

She thought about this for a minute. Maybe she didn't know the answer. Maybe it wasn't that hard, and she was afraid to say that Mom was silly for being so emotionally paralyzed by the accident.

"I don't know why some things are harder than others, Clover, but I do know that I care that this thing was hard for your mom."

"So you've known about all of this for a long time?" I asked.

"Yes. Remember when you came to walk the dog the first time, and you were so surprised that I would show myself without having my hair and makeup done?" she asked.

"I do remember. That started me thinking about a lot of things actually," I said.

"Well I love something called transparency. I love to help people be who God created them to be. Your mom started coming to the morning Bible study, and as I learned her story, I thought she would benefit from being in another small group where we focus on body image."

"I got a Bible one night after Alpha Omega," I said, "but Mom is the one who has been using it. She started to read Esther and loved it. I honestly thought she would go to Bible study and hate it because it would be too deep for her."

"And what about you? Have you been hating Bible study?" she asked.

"Me?" Mrs. Belle had turned the focus on me too quickly, and I wasn't ready for it. "I did hate it at first, but I craved it at the same time." Mrs. Belle nodded like she knew exactly what I was talking about. "I liked how you talked about Jesus."

I told her that there was something I was more afraid of than Mom changing, and I didn't even have to tell her what that was. She already knew.

"You're afraid of changing too?" she asked.

"Yes."

I told her that I tried to apply what I learned at Alpha Omega. I told her about Audrey and Nat and how, once I got to know them, I actually started to like them. Then I told her about the bargain I had made with God and how after last night, it was time to fulfill my end of it.

When I was finished, she left for a minute and came back with a ring and some paper and a pencil. She put the ring on the bench beside us, then wrote for a couple minutes with great caution.

"I listened to everything you said, Clover. I wrote your words down on paper. Perhaps the hardest thing about starting a relationship with Jesus is that we feel we have to be someone else. This prayer uses your exact words. Talking with him is like talking with a friend. Maybe it will take the fear away if you know what you will say ahead of time?"

She gave me the piece of paper and it said, "Hey, Jesus. I was just talking with Mrs. Belle about all the things in my heart. I made a bargain with you, but I'm scared of completing my end of it. I want to have a relationship with you, but I don't know what will happen if I do. The whole idea of mercy scares me, but I've seen that loving hard people is good and even addicting. I do want your mercy. I want your forgiveness. I don't trust you with my whole heart yet, but I want to. I want to learn. Will you teach me? Will you send your Holy Spirit to me to be my forever

Helper? I can't do life on my own. I need you, In Jesus name, Amen."

"Do you feel like you could pray those words, Clover?" she asked.

"Maybe," which meant yes, and she knew it.

Mrs. Belle picked up the ring. It wasn't fancy, but it wasn't from a gumball machine either. It was solid and gold plated but simple. A perfect thin gold circle.

She explained, "When Jesus invites you to be in a relationship with him, it's like an engagement. If you say 'yes' and take the ring, that's sort of like a reminder that you are now His. You're taken by a gentleman who loves you very much.

"You can do whatever you want with the ring. Some girls make a necklace out of it. Others have mounted it on a special wall hanging. When you get baptized, it will be like the wedding ceremony with all your friends and family. It's a public acknowledgment of your new decision to be a disciple of Christ."

I held the ring in my hand and began my relationship with Christ right there in Mrs. Belle's backyard. She called Mr. Belle out to pray with me, too, and he joked that he was going to call the dog over to baptize me with licking. Mrs. Belle was adamant that he stop joking, which made him do it even more. I giggled that they were bantering like that over the occasion. It made the whole thing feel real and not so churchy.

"Do you have any questions before you go?" Mrs. Belle asked.

"Nope." I started to leave, and then I figured I could use this opportunity to ask about The Challenge.

"There IS one thing. When do I know if I did The Challenge right? When will I know if I can go to Disneyland? I haven't given my stuff away yet, but I have a plan. Should I write a report at the end?" It was a question that was long overdue.

Mrs. Belle chuckled as though I were being naïve.

"Can you name the challenges thus far?" she asked.

"Well ... we've had the give in secret one and the light one. There was the love your enemies one that rocked my world the most. This month was find treasure ...." My voice trailed off. I said the words, "find treasure" as I looked at my ring. I lifted it up as if to say, "DUH!"

She smiled. "You've certainly found treasure! The point was to be challenged out of your comfort zone so that you would be softened and consider Jesus, Clover. I'd say you've ... considered him!"

"So, I'm going to Disneyland?" The reality hit me.

"That was always the plan, regardless of how The Challenge went for you." She confessed.

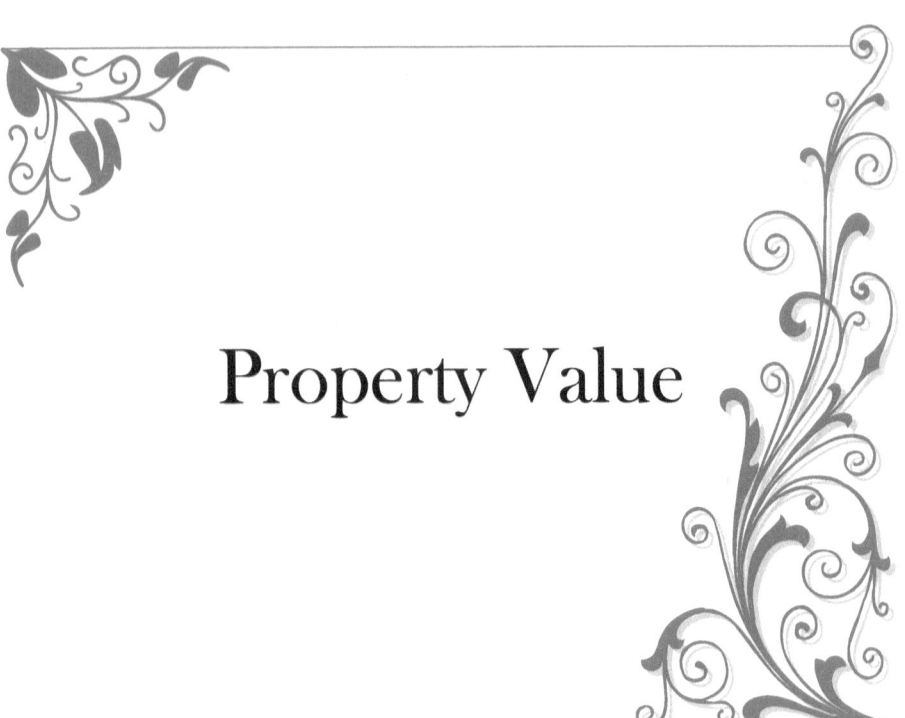

Property Value

Ever since we gave Nat and Audrey the forbidden T-shirts, they walked down the halls with more confidence, and our group of three decided to break away from our Alpha Omega lunch table to sit with them. We called it the Perfect Table. We even called it that in front of Nat and Audrey, and they took it as a compliment. If they ever decided to study the Sermon on the Mount with Mrs. Belle, we might be in trouble.

There was now a rhythm to our lunch routine. We'd open our lunches and then stick the food that we hated in the middle and swap for what we liked.

Audrey was actually quite the good listener when you got to know her. Talking too much was a nervous response, and once she had confidence in our friendship, sitting with her was a lot of fun. As far as Nat goes, once we broke the rules and gave her a T-shirt, she showed us her softer side.

The most painful part of being their new friend was watching how they interacted with the rest of the school and seeing their rough edges. Other kids made fun of Audrey, and I had to either stand up for her, or join in. Sometimes I chose well, other times I didn't.

History class was the worst for me. Since the beginning of the year, the seating chart was set, and each student sat according to their social class, like Monopoly property. We had each staked our social claim.

Audrey sat to the right, in the front row by the teacher. She was Baltic Avenue for $60. I was all the way to the left middle edge and sat by some other lower upper class properties: New York, Tennessee, and St. James for $180.

In front of me was Rudy Mendoza, Wes Coltrain, and Steve Erickson. They were all friends with the sports kids, so they were upper middle class properties: Marvin Gardens, Ventnor Avenue, and Atlantic Avenue for $260. These kids would talk to me occasionally, and it gave me quite a rush. It almost felt like Kentucky Avenue for $220.

Then there were the high-end property football players in the back left, behind me. They were rowdy enough to get attention, but not bad enough to get expelled from school. Chris Harper (Park Place $350) walked into class once with half his eyebrows shaved off. Rudy and Steve cracked up because they knew the backstory. I desperately wanted to know but would never ask. I made sure I had a book every day, and I would pretend to read so that I could listen to their stories and feel like I was in their group of friends. If I could repeat a Boardwalk story at the lunch table, then I felt like Illinois Avenue for $240.

In February, I found out how much I was personally worth. In Los Angeles, Valentine's Day was the day when girls got things delivered to them in class from their parents and friends—and possibly boys. So the week before, I always found that I was never quite myself. I wore a bit more makeup and laughed harder at every joke a boy told.

Evidently it was obvious because whenever we watched a show on Animal Planet about birds that primped their feathers to attract a mate, my brother would say, "Hey, there's Clover the week of Valentine's Day!" I hated him for it.

The Monday before Valentine's Day, Rudy Mendoza wore a nice brown leather jacket to school. While our teacher, Mr. Miner, was droning on and on to Audrey about how much he loved his summers off, I overheard the boys making fun of CSU for being the teacher's pet. I was thinking more about my desperation to win their favor than I was about Audrey's feelings.

I pulled out a piece of paper and drew a round face that took up the whole paper. Then I drew a giant mouth that took up almost the whole face. Inside the mouth I drew a picture of a ship and named it the Titanic. I wrote CSU on the top of the page with an arrow pointing to the face.

Just when I finished the degrading picture, I heard a HUGE sound right in front of me. On the back of Rudy's leather jacket was a spit wad the size of his whole back. Rudy and I turned around and looked at Chris Harper, who was laughing hysterically at his good work.

Batting my eyes and trying to look super cute, I said, "That is so gross! How did you get that giant piece of paper so wet like that? You could NOT have put that whole thing in your mouth— it's too big!" They weren't listening because they were laughing as loud as they could without distracting the teacher. We all knew that when Mr. Miner stopped his story, class would begin.

When the teacher said, "OK guys, what is this?" I thought he was talking about the laughing boys. Instead, he was holding a piece of paper in his hand. Out of the corner of my eye, I noticed that the picture I had drawn of my sweet friend Audrey was gone.

My face went hot and I looked at the boys to my right. They gave me a look of guilty pleasure. In the fifteen seconds that I'd been distracted by the spit wad, they had passed around the picture, which ended up in the teacher's hands.

Audrey wanted to see it, too, and Mr. Miner stupidly handed it to her. I was mortified. I never meant for her to see it!

She looked at the giant head with the Titanic in the mouth and put her head down. One of the boys called over to her, "The ship should've been called, S.S. Audrey!" She pretended she thought it was funny, but I knew she didn't. I felt utterly guilty and totally caught.

The boys never said that I was the one who drew the picture, but when no one was looking, they all gave me pats on the back and congratulated me for humiliating my friend and giving them a good laugh. I guess that's what popularity felt like. Each pat on the back encouraged my dream that I would get a special delivery from one of them on Valentine's Day. The boys treated me like I could hang out with them on Park Place, but my soul felt like I should go directly to jail.

In Hiding

I felt bad when our teacher handed Audrey the picture, but eating lunch with her was even worse. She held her uneaten baloney sandwich in one hand and cried over the terrible person who would do such a thing. The terrible person—who was sitting right next to her.

She showed us the picture, "The worst part is that the whole class passed it around, and all the boys were in on it. It was like the whole class was making fun of me. Well, not you, Clover. I know you wouldn't do that."

I looked at her sadly, which she translated as compassion.

"I'm sure you know who did it, but you don't have to tell me unless you want to," she said.

"I'm not sure it would make you feel better if you knew," I said with certainty.

"Probably not." Then, with tears in her eyes, she said, "I just want to know what's wrong with me? Is there something wrong with me?"

"There's nothing wrong with you, Audrey," Nat chimed in. "Whoever did that is a jerk, and they deserve to die!" Nat was not full of grace about the whole thing.

"Actually, I think we can tell a lot about the person who drew this by looking at it," Twinkle said.

"We can?" said Audrey, "like what?"

Twinkle put the paper on the table where we could all see it. "Well, for instance, someone drew the face with soft features. If this were a boy they would have drawn the eyes and nose more buggy or something because boys like to be gross. The Titanic is a ship that was thought to be one thing, but in the end it was the exact opposite. Maybe the person is still trying to decide how they feel about you. Maybe the person who drew this is a girl, and the ship represents her heart, which is not quite on solid ground yet." When Twinkle said that, she looked right at me.

Audrey looked thoughtful, "Hmmm. That's interesting. Maybe it wasn't one of the boys in the back. Maybe it was one of the cheerleaders that sit around me."

My eyes grew wide. Did Twinkle know it was me? I couldn't bear it anymore. "I'll sit by you in class tomorrow, Audrey."

"But we have a seating chart, and you can't move," she said.

"I know," I said, "but after today, I feel like taking a stand and making a change in that class. Something needs to be done. You deserve to be treated better than that." It was true. She did, and I knew that now. Lesson learned.

What I needed to do was make sure Audrey was distracted enough in class, so those boys could never tell her what I did. I had to make sure she never knew the truth.

The thought of her finding out that I had drawn the picture made me sick. On the other hand, the thought of spending every moment of my life worried that she would find out also made me sick. I was stuck in my own skin, and I couldn't get out.

I wondered if this was how Mom felt for the thirteen years she wore a wig and locked her bedroom door, hiding from the truth of the accident. I understood for the first time why she hid, but I had no doors to lock. Having a secret is the loneliest of all places.

On the bus ride home, I sat with my head against the window. "Are you okay, Clover?" Twinkle asked.

"I don't feel well. I just want to go to bed." I didn't even turn to look at her.

Twinkle and Sara talked the whole bus ride and let me be.

When I got home, I went straight to the comfort of my troll doll room, and I stared at the ring that Mrs. Belle had given me. I decided to keep it in my pocket so that when there was an opportune time, I could give it back to her. That seemed like the only right thing to do. I didn't deserve it.

Twinkle

I got up the next morning to walk the dog. Not because I wanted to make more money, but because I wanted to leave the ring on Mrs. Belle's front porch. The thought of giving it back to her in person was too shameful. She would ask me why, and I would probably start crying and tell her the whole story, and I couldn't face that. I wasn't ready to be a Christian. I wasn't good enough.

The walk to Mrs. Belle's house felt hard, like I was straining forward, pressing myself through something thick. My soul felt like a massive glob of dirty toilet paper trying to get through the pipes, but there wasn't enough water to push it through.

When I was almost to Mrs. Belle's house, I heard someone call my name.

"Clover! Wait up!" It was Twinkle.

"What are you doing here?" I asked.

"I'm going to walk with you this morning. I think you need a friend," she said.

I didn't say anything.

"Clover, did you draw that picture?" Twinkle asked, and I immediately started crying. I didn't want to cry, but the second she said that, it was like someone flushed my pipes, and the rush of water started to move the dirty toilet paper out of my soul.

I sat down in the middle of the street. I was a mess. I sobbed for a long time. Probably only thirty seconds, but it seemed like forever. Twinkle sat with me, and when a car came, we moved to the curb.

When my crying was under control and I could talk, I started to open up, "Yesterday at lunch I could tell that you knew I was the one who drew the picture."

"I didn't know until the bus ride home."

"Really?" I was surprised. "But what you said about the Titanic and the girl who drew it .... I thought you were ratting me out."

"Oh no! I was making stuff up to comfort Audrey. I was trying to help her see that the girl who drew the picture had feelings too," she said.

I pointed to my shirt that was wet from my tears and snot and said, "The girl who drew that picture most definitely has feelings too."

"Last year, before we moved here," Twinkle said, "I was involved in something much worse. I know exactly how you feel, Clover."

"It's hard to imagine you doing something hurtful," I said.

"Well then, you need to listen to THIS!" she said, as though her story would prove me wrong. "Two years ago, when I started my first year of middle school, life was pretty perfect for me. I had a great group of friends, I was well respected by my teachers, and my parents spoke well of me.

"That all changed one night when my dad was going to take me to my neighbor's baseball game. He was the coach and wanted me to go, but I changed my mind at the last minute and decided to stay home.

"Mom had one of my teachers over who had been a family friend since I was little. They thought I was at the baseball game, so they sat at our kitchen table and talked about Mom things. I heard them talking and, like any curious eleven-year-old, I sat at the top of the stairs to listen to their conversation.

"BIG mistake. My teacher said some things that I shouldn't have heard. I desperately wanted to go back to my room, but at the same time, I desperately wanted to keep listening because knowing a secret can be so thrilling. In the end, I told myself that if I got up, the floor might creak, and they would know that I was eavesdropping.

"When I went back to school, I made all my friends pinky swear not to tell anyone what I was about to say. When they put their pinkies in the middle, I trusted that they would keep it between us.

"With every word that came out of my mouth about our teacher friend, I felt like I was spilling her guts all over the table. I stopped halfway through and my friends were all like, 'Twinkle! You can't stop now. We HAVE to know. You made us curious! PLEASE PLEASE,' they begged. 'We won't tell.' They promised, and I foolishly believed them. So I told.

"My friends all kept their promises not to tell, except to that one person that *they* made pinky swear not to say a word. And the other people they told, and they also pinky swore. Until our beloved family friend's secret got to the school administration. Evidently, her little secret was against school policy, and she got fired. And who was the only person she told her little secret to?"

"Your mom," I answered before she could.

"So guess who got the blame for getting her fired and having her reputation ruined?" she asked.

"Your mom." It was an obvious answer, but I said it out loud so she didn't have to.

"Yep. My mom." She confirmed. "She was sad and confused and didn't know what had happened. She was innocent.

"The day my teacher got fired, I went home on the bus, and I pressed my face against the window. When I saw you doing the same thing, I knew that you had drawn the picture, and it brought me back to that place in life that I never wanted to go back to."

"What did you do, Twinkle?" I understood her choices. They were the same dead end choices that I faced.

"I told the truth," she said without joy. "I told my mom what I had done, and she made me face our friend and tell her too."

"Oh my GOSH! You had to TELL her?" My emotional reflexes were gagging.

"I did." She offered no more than that, and I could see the writing on the wall.

"It didn't end well, did it?" I wasn't sure I wanted to know.

"No, it didn't. I'd like to say that it was worth it. In one sense it was better because I didn't have to protect myself from being found out. But on the other hand, there is a family friend out there who doesn't speak to us anymore. She is jobless and believes that I ruined her life. That doesn't feel good." She had one hand on her knee and was doodling on the street with a stick.

"I am so sorry, Twinkle," I offered.

"Thanks," she said. "I get that you don't want to tell Audrey that you drew that picture, and yet, there's a part of you that does."

It was good to hear Twinkle's story. Everything seemed so easy for her, and I had assumed that she was the perfect Christian and had it all together.

"So what do I do?" I asked Twinkle. It was the same question I asked Sara earlier in the year under different circumstances.

"I don't know what you do, Clover. What helped me was to memorize our Alpha Omega verse for this month. Matthew 7:7 *Ask, and it will be given to you; seek, and you will find; knock, and it will be opened to you.*" She spouted off the scripture without skipping a beat.

"I asked God to help our friend forgive me like Lisa at Alpha Omega forgave those girls. My only hope is that what Jesus says is true," she said.

The bus passed by us.

"Oooops. I guess we missed the bus," I said apathetically. This seemed way more important than school. I hoped Mom wouldn't be mad that she would have to drive me now.

Mrs. Belle came out of her house and motioned for us to come over to her, "Hey girls, why don't you get in my car. I'll take you home, and if you can get ready quickly, I'll take you to school."

"Oh yeah, I sort of forgot we were sitting right outside of Mrs. Belle's house," Twinkle said.

She dropped me off first. I went to my room and before I took a quick shower, I put my ring back on my dresser.

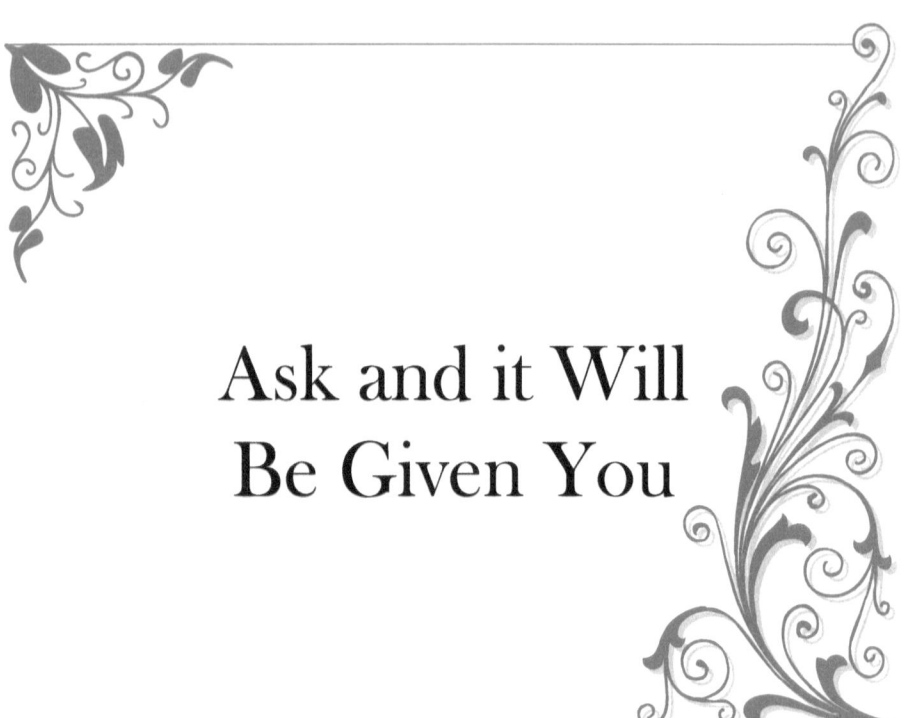

Ask and it Will
Be Given You

Thursday was Valentine's Day, which was a relief because I had Alpha Omega to look forward to on a day that could've been really lonely and depressing.

I sat by Audrey in history class all week, and everyone in the class—except probably me and Audrey—seemed to have forgotten about my little drawing stunt. That was helpful. The only thing that reminded me about it was my own guilt.

Alpha Omega could not have come soon enough.

We had already had a couple talks on the theme, *Ask and it will be given you,* so we spent the evening doing an exercise to help us understand prayer a little more. Mrs. Belle had everyone go up front where there was plenty of room for all fifty girls to move around.

The ninth graders spread out around us, and the only instruction we had was to apply the scripture for the month, Matthew 7:7 *Ask and it will be given you, seek and you shall find, knock and the door will be opened to you.*

We weren't allowed to gather in groups or work together, so I went over to Lisa. The scripture's first command was to ask, so I thought I would try that.

But I didn't know what to ask. Other girls were talking and laughing and running to other helpers. "What am I supposed to do?" I asked Lisa. It was a good starter question. She put her hand in her pocket to get something.

She opened her hand and there was a rock. I squinted and pushed my eyebrows down to convey my lack of understanding. I saw some other girls wandering around to other ninth graders, so I chose another girl, too.

I stood in front of her and asked, "Do you also have a rock?" She showed me a rock and nodded her head yes.

I moved on to another ninth grade helper. I asked, "Does everyone have a rock?" She didn't budge. I looked around to see most of the girls joking around and having fun. I didn't think it was so fun. I stared at the girl in front of me. "Do YOU have a rock?"

I hated puzzles. My brain didn't think that way. If people gave me directions, I could do it, but you have to tell me what to do. Don't make me try to figure it out. Or don't make me wait for it. I hate waiting.

I asked the girl in front of me, who I didn't really know, if she had a rock, and she did. Every girl had one. I stayed with her and asked, "Where did everyone go?" She didn't answer. I thought a little more. By this time I was the last one in the room. All the girls had even moved on to some other mysterious thing, and I almost started crying. Out of desperation I asked, "Will you help me find out where I'm supposed to go?" Her eyes lit up and she said, "YES, of course I'll help you, Clover."

Never mind how she knew my name. She probably wouldn't tell me anyway. Dumb game. She put her hand in her pocket and handed me a piece of paper that said, *Room 156*. I didn't know where the heck that room was.

THE CHALLENGE *by Wendy Everts*

In the hallway I saw another ninth grade helper, and I showed her the piece of paper. "Can you please help me find this room?"

"Sure!" she said, and she pointed down the hallway. At the end of the hall was another helper who showed me the next step, and so on and so on until I got to Room 156. I had no idea the church was so huge!

There was a little table with paper and a pencil in the hall outside Room 156. On the top of the paper was written, *What do you really need right now?*

That wasn't a hard question. I wrote, *I really want …* but then I erased it. No, that wasn't right. I didn't just want it. I needed help. I needed someone to help me understand what to do about Audrey. The longer I waited to tell her that I drew that picture, the more hurt she would be if she found out it was me.

The hall was full of other girls writing on their own pieces of paper. I was done with the assignment and didn't know what to do next. The other girls sat in front of their own doors, writing. No one had gotten up to leave yet.

I looked at the door and thought about the third part of the verse, *KNOCK and the door will be opened to you.* I got up and timidly knocked on the door. I felt silly in front of all those girls. If I was wrong, I would feel really stupid.

The door opened and Mrs. Belle said, "Welcome! I've been expecting you!" Relief washed over me that someone had answered. I had the feeling of déjà vu, like this was the day I first knocked on her door to sell her something for our fundraiser, although that seemed like forever ago.

The room was full of comfortable nap couches and pictures of people being welcomed. One picture I particularly liked was a warm charcoal blue color. It showed a child being held by a safe, strong man.

Mrs. Belle didn't say anything. She sat down on one of the couches, and I sat too. "You probably want to see what I wrote on my paper," I said, holding it tightly.

"Do YOU want me to see, Clover?" she asked.

"You can read it if you want to, I guess." I handed her the paper tentatively.

She read it and asked if this had anything to do with what Twinkle and I had been talking about outside her house the other day. I told her the whole story, and she listened just like I imagined that man in the picture would.

She didn't give me any magical advice, like I expected. "Whenever I get in a pickle with someone and need to have a scary talk with them, I ask God to make things right in his own timing. If you put him in charge of things, then you can let it go and relax."

I wasn't so sure. I reminded her that I was new at this whole faith thing, and she asked me one question that put me in my place. "When you made a bargain with God earlier this year and asked him why your mom wore a wig, what happened, Clover?"

"God gave me what I wanted." That was two months ago and I had already forgotten. "Oh yeah," I said.

"He answered your prayer, didn't he?" She reminded me, "It was a HUGE prayer. He could certainly answer this one."

"What do I ask for?" I asked.

"How did you get to this room?" she asked.

"Not easily. I hated that, by the way," I said.

She laughed. Her question was still unanswered.

"I guess, in the end, I asked for help," I said.

"YES!!! That's it Clover. Tell God everything and then ask for help. Then wait for it." She had way more enthusiasm than I did.

We had prayed together once before when I accepted the ring on her back porch, but that was different. She had given me the words to say.

"Let's pray about it," she encouraged. "You can repeat after me, and then use your own words when you feel comfortable. I'll help you."

For the first time ever, I prayed out loud with someone, and I didn't die. I told God about my story and how scared I was, and I told him that I needed help. Mrs. Belle prompted me and helped me be specific.

When we were done and headed out the door, she said, "Oh yeah, I almost forgot. Here Clover, Happy Valentine's Day." She handed me a sealed envelope.

I rolled my eyes, "You and your ENVELOPES!!!! I hate these things."

She laughed. "No, no. This time it's just a card. Don't worry."

Dad picked me up and asked what we did that night. I started to tell him and then said, "Wait. Have you done the exercise for *Ask and it will be given you?*" Our parents were doing the same studies that we were.

He got excited, "We did it at our last Bible study! We met at church before work with your mom's Tuesday morning study. The best part for me was that other couples came and volunteered as the helpers."

"When did you figure out you were supposed to knock?" I asked.

"What? What are you talking about?" he asked.

I told him about the rocks and the progression of events to the door. He told me that he and Mom did all of that.

"Then you just left after you filled out the paper?" I felt sad that they missed out on that.

"Well, yeah. We figured that the point was to understand what we need so that we could ask God for it, right?" He was confident about the lesson.

"But your paper had a room number on it, right?" I asked.

"Sure, but ... gosh, I didn't even THINK about knocking. What happens when you knock? Does God come out?" He laughed at his own joke.

"Haha, Dad ... no! Someone was in that room waiting for you!" I broke it to him bluntly.

"Seriously? I wonder who was behind our door. Did YOU knock?" he asked.

Not only did I rub it in that I knocked, I connected the dots and joked that it meant that I was better at following Jesus than he was.

He heard my joke but ignored it to talk about a bigger subject. "You know, Clover, I have been thinking about surprising your mom with something special for our anniversary next month."

"Really? Like what? A trip or something?" I loved the idea of surprising Mom.

"No, I think I want to get remarried as Christians and have a vow renewal service. I've been thinking about it ever since we took rings at Alpha Omega together," he said.

Dad wasn't normally romantic, so the idea excited the heck out of me,"SERIOUSLY?" I exclaimed. "Can I help you plan it, Dad? I have some great ideas. Give me a guest list and tell me what day, and Twinkle, Sara, and I will make the invitations. Can I surprise you with some things too?"

"You know I'm terrible at the planning. It was the only thing that I didn't ...." I wouldn't let him finish.

"You know what? How about I'll take care of everything. You just tell Mom that she's yours on your anniversary," I insisted.

"I don't want to put too much on you, Clover ...." I interrupted again. He was defenseless against my excitement about the whole thing.

"I promise, Dad. It won't be too much. I'll get my friends help me. Please? Pretty please ...." I said please over and over and batted my eyes real hard.

"Okay. I'll let you do it. But nothing fancy, alright? We don't have a lot of money," he urged.

"You forget! I've been walking Mrs. Belle's dog for four months! I've got a wad of cash! Don't you worry about a thing! YAY!!!!" He had no idea about the resources available to me.

We pulled into the driveway and went inside. Mom had decorated for Valentine's Day as a special surprise for me and my brother. There were candles on the table and red balloons tied to the chairs.

"Oh yeah," I said. "Happy Valentine's Day, Dad!"

After having some time with my family, I went to my room and opened my card. No challenges this time. Just a Valentine's Day card from Mrs. Belle telling me that she loved me. It was nice.

I checked the calendar to see what day Mom and Dad's anniversary fell on, and my heart sank. A Thursday. I was hoping that Mrs. Belle would be available to help me. After the lesson on *Ask, Seek, and Knock,* I felt bold enough to see if she would skip Alpha Omega for one night to help me. Ask and it will be given to you, right? I had nothing to lose!

Build Your
House on Rock

 ot only did Mrs. Belle like the idea of being involved with my parents' vow renewal, she liked the idea of it being on a Thursday night so that we could combine the two events.

The Alpha Omega team was always thinking of fun exercises and activities to help us apply scripture. Mrs. Belle thought my parents' renewal of vows was a perfect fit with our monthly theme. She suggested that the ceremony be a part of Alpha Omega, and I agreed, as long as Twinkle, Sara, and I could be in charge of the decorations and planning.

Their anniversary was in the middle of March, so we had four weeks to plan. We decided to meet at 6:30 AM because that was my usual time to walk the dog. That way Mom wouldn't suspect a thing. Twinkle rode her bike, and Sara and I walked to Mrs. Belle's house every morning that first week. We spent twenty-five minutes each day working on the details, and by Friday we knew what our different jobs were and what we needed to do to get ready.

Sara was going to make matching Sharpie tie-dye shirts for everyone so that all the girls in Alpha Omega would be wearing white with a splash of color. I was in charge of figuring out the sizes and buying supplies and decorations. My brother agreed to take me to the store to get the stuff I needed. Twinkle would send invitations and make sure everyone from my parents' Bible studies and Dad's work were there. Mrs. Belle collaborated with the worship team to have special music, and she asked Mr. Belle to perform the ceremony.

The worst part was that I couldn't let on at home that anything was going on. There were days that the stress got to be too much, and I was sure that Mom suspected that something was going on.

The week before the ceremony, Mrs. Belle gave everyone the scoop at Alpha Omega. Sara handed out the T-shirts and reminded everyone to hide them from Mrs. Mannerhouse, in case she came in to pick me up at the end of the evening. I talked to the group about the decorating logistics.

As a cover for the vow renewal ceremony, my parents had gotten a fake invitation in the mail to attend another parents' night for Alpha Omega, and Dad worked hard to convince Mom to go. I thought it would be the perfect way to get her there without blowing the secret, but she was dead set on having a different anniversary celebration, one that she would plan.

They argued for the first time in a long time—about the evening I had worked so hard to make special. I felt a little guilty that Dad had to put his foot down to convince Mom to go to something so unromantic.

"Tom, when we have other discussions, you listen really well to me, and we figure out what we are going to do toogethah! Why aren't you listening to me now?" she pleaded.

"If you felt listened to, would you do it my way?" he asked.

"Oh my gosh!" she shouted. "Why do we have to do it your way? Are you listening to yourself?"

"Okay, I'll listen ... what do you want to do that evening?" he said.

"I don't know, go to dinner or something romantic. Dancing maybe?" she said.

"I promise you," he said, "Alpha Omega is going to be WAY more romantic than that."

"You are making fun of me right now, aren't you Tom Mannahhouse!!!" She was incredulous.

"No, I'm serious," he answered. "What happens at Alpha Omega will be a lot more romantic."

"Why? If you are serious, then you have to tell me. Why is it going to be more romantic? Hmmmm?" Mom could be pretty insistent. He was backed into a corner.

I stiffened. If he told her what we'd planned, I would just die. He seemed deep in thought.

"What's the theme of the month, Maggie Ann?" he asked.

"Build your house on a rock." She answered correctly.

"And what," he asked, "is the point of the scripture this month?"

"To do what scripture says," she recited, "so we build our lives on Christ. When we do what scripture says, it makes our lives strong and unshakable, like building our house on a rock." Her voice was a bit impersonal.

"That's what I want on our anniversary, Maggie Ann. I want to go to Alpha Omega and celebrate our anniversary. I want to hold hands with you and maybe sit in the back and dance during worship. I want our life to be about doing the word of God toogethah!" He grabbed her hand and touched his pointer fingers with hers then held her hand, which made her break into a smile.

Home run, Dad, I thought.

He hugged her and danced with her a little bit, taking charge of the moment and swinging her around to his humming. A little taste of what was to come. "You can't do THAT at a restaurant, now can you, Maggie Ann?"

"Okay, okay, I'll go," she surrendered.

I breathed a sigh of relief. "Thank God," I said aloud.

"But I want you to take me to dinner Friday night for a REAL celebration." The request was reasonable.

"Maggie Ann, if you will go to Alpha Omega with me Thursday night, I will take you anywhere you want on Friday." He kissed her hand and sealed the deal.

And that was the end of that.

Focusing on my schoolwork on Thursday was impossible. I was so excited about all of our plans and the surprise for Mom that I couldn't eat all day. If it had been up to Dad, he would've arranged a simple ceremony at our house to renew their vows, but that just didn't seem right for all that had changed for us.

Everything needed to be perfect. Mrs. Belle agreed to tell my parents that she needed me for the afternoon, so they wouldn't ask me any questions. Twinkle's parents helped get us to the ceremony location early, so we could decorate. When we had finished, we stepped back to look at all that we had done and hoped it would be beautiful, but then again, we wouldn't really know until dark.

Mom and Dad drove to the church that evening, but when they got there, it was dark and empty.

"I thought Alpha Omega was meeting here tonight, Tom? What's going on? Do we have the wrong night?" she asked.

"No, this is exactly the right night," he said. The parking lot was empty—except for one car. Dad drove over to it, and the driver got out of the limo.

Dad said, "Hold on, Maggie Ann. Don't get out quite yet." He jumped out and went to her side of the car, opened the door, and offered her his hand.

"Oh Tom, is THIS why you were so insistent on us coming to Alpha Omega? What is going on? Are we getting in that limo?" She was starting to get excited.

They slid into the limo that was stocked with special drinks, and they poured each other a glass of fresh squeezed limeade from a crystal pitcher that sat on ice. They clinked glasses and said, "To us. To new life in Jesus and building our house on a rock. Cheers!"

The driver toured them around town long enough to make Mom wonder where the heck they would end up. He finally drove through the park until they reached a place where they could see a soft glow coming through the trees.

"What is this place, Tom? What are we doing?" Dad just smiled. He was going to let her wait and find out for herself.

He took her hand and led her through the trees toward the glow. They held hands and walked slowly. I was waiting and watching in the dark, so I could cue the musicians at the perfect time. Plus, I wanted to see Mom's face.

When they came through the trees, they turned down a short lane that was all lit up like a church aisle with five thousand circular glow sticks. Fifteen volunteers had chucked them up in the trees this afternoon. They were uneven, but it didn't matter.

Mom gasped. "It's beautiful, Tom!"

The worship leaders were singing, and at the end of the lane, the natural altar was waiting for them. All the girls from Alpha Omega, my parent's friends from Bible study, and Dad's co-workers were lined up on either side of the walkway. The girls from Alpha Omega were out in front like a line of bridesmaids, wearing the T-shirts Sara had made.

Mom looked around in wonder. Dad did too. He had let me plan the whole thing, but I hadn't told him anything, only where to go and what time. He had no idea what we had planned. Tears streamed down both their faces, and I had to admit, I was getting a bit teary myself.

When they got to the altar at the end of the path, I stood in front of them, waiting. I handed Dad a little box. My first present. He looked at the tiny box that was like so many little boxes he had held and sold on TV, but could never buy. He opened it, and inside was a beautiful diamond ring that I knew would fit Mom.

"Clover!" they both gasped. For a minute, it looked like they wouldn't accept this gift.

I put their hands together and walked away. Dad hesitated and then surrendered to the gift. He got down on one knee. He took her hand and said, "Maggie Ann Mannerhouse, would you marry me all over again?"

"Yes!" she blurted. That was all she could say because she was crying so hard. He held the ring tight, as if he were afraid he would lose it, and it sparkled in the soft glow of the lights.

All of his friends from Bible study came forward and stood on Dad's left. Wigless women with varying degrees of hair stood to Mom's right.

Mr. and Mrs. Belle came up to take charge of the ceremony. She began to read the scripture for the month of March, and I watched my parents mouth the words along with her, as if they had them memorized.

> "Matthew 7:24-27 *Everyone then who hears these words of mine and does them will be like a wise man who built his house on the rock. And the rain fell, and the floods came, and the winds blew and beat on that house, but it did not fall, because it had been founded on the rock. And everyone who hears these words of mine and does not do them will be like a foolish man who built his house on the sand. And the rain fell, and the floods came, and the winds blew and beat against that house, and it fell, and great was the fall of it.*"

After the reading, Mr. Belle spoke about the scripture. I was excited to hear what he would say since I'd been learning from Mrs. Belle the whole year.

"We are here tonight because Tom wanted to renew his vows with Maggie Ann. We are really glad she said yes!" I giggled. I liked Mr. Belle.

He went on. "Jesus pleads with his followers to DO what he has said. If you do, you will be like a house built on rock. Jesus said that if you don't do what he's said, you will be like a house built on sand.

"Building your house on the rock takes hard work. Doing what Jesus says takes hard work.

"Let me remind you, Tom and Maggie Ann, what we've asked you to do this year. We asked you not to buy anything for a whole month. We challenged you to give everything in secret, to be a light, and to love hard people. We invited you to consider giving your life to Jesus and to learn how to pour your heart out in prayer and ask for what you need." It was clear that Mr. Belle knew my parents well.

He spoke about every part of The Challenge, which brought back my own feelings of both struggle and delight. I was taken back to the days of talking to Audrey and finding out Nat's name. I remembered making Audrey and Nat T-shirts like ours. I agreed with Mr. Belle that it would have been much easier for me to stay at my Alpha Omega lunch table and just stick to myself this year.

Mr. Belle looked directly at Mom and Dad. "In a moment, I am going to help you renew your vows, but it's up to you to build your marriage on that rock. No one can do that for you. I think you are ready because you have already started to do that."

Mr. Belle shared examples of how Mom and Dad had grown over this past year and chosen hard things. A lot of things I didn't even know. A new respect for them rose up in me as I learned about some choices they had made.

When it was finally time for the vows, Mr. Belle asked my parents to hold hands, and he asked Dad for the ring. He took the ring out of the box, and Mom took off her original ring and put it in the box, so they wouldn't lose it.

Mr. Belle asked Dad to repeat after him, and before he could say anything else, Mom shouted out, "WAIT!"

This didn't seem like a good sign. Had she changed her mind?

Then Mom did something that no one, not even in their wild-est dreams, would expect. She took a deep breath, put her hand up to her head, and yanked off her wig. She turned her balding head to face all of us and handed that wig to Lisa, who clutched it like a maid of honor holding the bride's bouquet.

Dad gasped proudly, "MAGGIE ANN!"

"Okay, now, Tom," she said. "Now say your vows to me. Let's start building our house on rock right here. No hiding."

She turned to all of us and said, "So this is me. This is what I really look like."

All the balding bridesmaids dabbed their eyes, remembering the first time that they, too, showed themselves in public without their hair.

Dad announced, "Even more beautiful than when I married you the first time."

We crowded around to hear them renew their vows.

"I, Tom, take you, Maggie Ann, to be my lawfully wedded wife. For richer and for poorer, in sickness and in health, for bet-ter or worse, from this day forward." Mr. Belle added on a spe-cial part for him to repeat, "To build the Kingdom, to help each other grow in faith, and to live life digging deep into the rock and choosing the things that will give us a solid life. To give in secret, to choose forgiveness, to love hard people, and to ask God for what we need."

After their vows, Mrs. Belle grabbed two crystal goblets and some bread and juice. Mom and Dad took communion, then passed it around to all of us.

Then Mr. Belle made a surprise announcement, "We have a kiddie pool behind us that's filled with water. Since you two haven't been baptized, would you like to take the opportunity to do that now?"

The worship team led us in song, and Mom and Dad were baptized. Then Dad grabbed my mother and danced with her.

Unapologetic and free. Sara sang the song that she had sung the night they'd taken their rings and committed to follow Jesus.

Twinkle and I raced to the kiddie pool. We took off our shoes, hiked up our skirts, and stomped in the water. Several people sang and splashed while Dad sweetly held Mom in his arms.

When the songs were over, Mom and Dad went back down the lane, and we did our best to blow bubbles in their faces, but the soap was too thin. Our bubble wands dripped and made us all a sticky mess, so we gave up and just clapped for them.

They got back in the limo and headed home, where the RV waited in our driveway. I had arranged for it to be delivered to our house, and my brother decorated it with a big sign that said, **Honeymoon Suite.** We filled it with the rest of my presents from the fundraising catalog: A toaster oven, a blender, and a deck of cards I bought myself. I had planned to use the RV for my eighth grade graduation, but I figured this was a far better cause.

It was the first night that my brother and I had spent alone without our parents, and we actually got along. If all brothers and sisters have a moment in time that sets them on the trajectory toward becoming friends, then that was our moment.

We went into our parents' once forbidden room, got out the photo albums, and looked at all the pictures. We talked about high school because I was starting to get nervous about that.

Most importantly, we talked about how cool it was that Mom and Dad were different. We plotted to tease them that they were going through 'the change.' We used all the terms they used when they teased us about going through puberty. "Wow, your voice is different. Someone is going through 'the change'! Dad, it looks like you are noticing Mom these days. Is someone going through 'the change'?!"

We never actually teased our parents like we said we would, but we had a good bonding moment over it. From that night forward, we were on the same team: The Mannerhouse Team.

Use What You Have to Be Welcomed

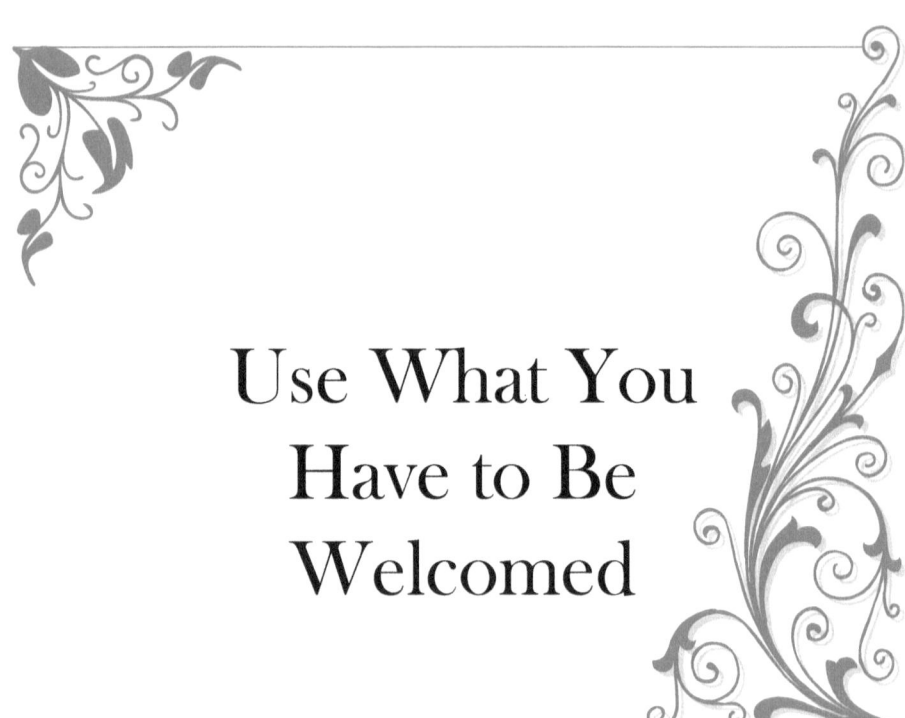

$\mathcal{W}$e still had two and a half months of school left. We were set to go to Disneyland in May, over Memorial Day weekend, and I couldn't wait.

Besides spending money on Christmas presents and my parents' ceremony, I had saved up $525 from walking the dog all year. In truth, I had earned far more than money from walking the dog. I had gained Sara as a friend, and that would stay with me forever. Literally. She was treasure. I didn't know much about heaven, but if it were a true place, I wanted to live by Sara when I got there.

On the first Thursday night in April, we started our new theme, *Use What You Have to Be Welcomed*. Before Mrs. Belle started the talk or read any scripture, she passed around a hat and we drew out numbers. We had to find the seat with our number on it, which mixed us all up and forced us to sit by someone different. Sara, Twinkle, and I grabbed onto each other and pretended that we were incapable of separating. Eventually we did the right thing and parted.

Our assignment was to share our answer to this question with the girl next to us: What is most important to you—money, time, or your favorite things? Out of those, which one is most precious to you?

The girl next to me was someone I sat with at lunch sometimes, and we agreed that the most precious thing was our money.

Suddenly there was a commotion as Lisa ran into the room. The bells on her outfit distracted us from our conversations. She squeezed by the folks seated in a middle row and said, "Pardon me, pardon me, pardon me!" There was a great slapping noise as she smacked a wad of green papers into her hand, then she threw a ton of bills up in the air that sprayed everywhere.

Mayhem and uproar arose from all of us when we realized that there were real hundred dollar bills flying everywhere. I grabbed three. Mrs. Belle made us give away our extra ones to those who didn't get one.

Calm was not a word I would use to describe the room. Having money in our hands made us hyper. Mrs. Belle stood upfront, unhurried to speak. After a while, things calmed down.

"Now I want you to talk with your neighbor about what you will buy with this money." She encouraged us to share again with the same neighbor.

My friend didn't have any trouble thinking about how to spend her money. "Nike socks, converse high tops, a Build-a-Bear, and then I'll spend the rest on candy. I'm going to spend it all!" She tapped her feet excitedly and smelled her money.

I had a little more trouble. I already had a stack of bills in my room that I was having trouble spending. "I don't know," I said. "Maybe I would see what kind of jewelry my dad was selling at the shopping network and buy a pretty ring." There were always pretty rings available on his channel for a reasonable price.

"Do you want to know The Challenge for this month?" Mrs. Belle asked. We hadn't even heard the scripture yet. "Sometime this month, use the money in your hand to buy what your friend just told you she wants, then give it to her."

That was it. She didn't explain more. We had money in our hands and an invitation to spend it on the person next to us.

To remind myself of what she wanted, I said out loud, "Nike socks, Converse high tops, a Build-a-Bear, and candy. What size shoe do you wear?" I asked her.

"Size seven," she said, then asked, "What size ring do you wear?"

"I don't know," I said.

"Here put this on." She gave me her ring and I put it on. It fit just right.

"Five and a half," she said. "Great. I am going to get you something beautiful."

The hundred dollars was in my hand. Couldn't I just keep it and add it to my pile of money at home? Why couldn't I choose my own ring and buy it for myself? There was a reason. Mrs. Belle always had some reason.

"Girls," Mrs. Belle said, "I want to introduce you to an actor friend of mine, Max. He is going to perform a monologue that he wrote based on our scripture tonight, Luke 16:1-13."

Max was an old guy and with great effort, he came up front. I was curious to see this old guy act out scripture.

"Good evening!" he said.

"Good evening," we greeted back.

"Let me introduce myself. I am Max, and I am a business owner. Anyone here ever owned a business?" We thought he was acting, so no one said anything. He repeated himself, "I said, anyone here own a business?" He was loud and animated for being ancient.

The answer was no, of course. We were in middle school, after all.

"Well I do, and let me tell you, it is tough stuff. People steal from you all the time." He got into his groove, and I could tell that he was an actor. A good one.

"Oh, you thought I meant the customers were stealing from me I bet! No! I'm talking about my employees!" Max was funny the way he talked.

"Like, this one guy. His name was Tyler, but we called him 'Sly Ty' because I had to watch 'em. I suspected he had sticky fingers, so I put up a camera near my cash register to prove he was stealing from me.

"This one day I went out of town, and when I came back, I watched the videos and found out that bad 'ole Sly Ty was taking money out of MY REGISTER!!! That dirty duck ...." He muttered out of the side of his mouth. We laughed.

"I caught him red-handed. Boy was I mad, and he knew it too. He could tell I was going to fire him, so do you know what Sly Ty did?"

"WHAT?" we said loudly. His story was so genuine we all believed him. We wondered what a guy like Sly Ty would do if he was about to be fired.

"He went to the home of one of my customers."

Now Max became Sly Ty. He got up and walked as though he were a confident twenty-year-old. The guy wasn't really decrepit and old, he was ACTING!

Sly Ty went to one of the girls in the front seat and asked in a slick, cunning voice, "Hey YOU owe Max money for that TV you bought from him. How much do you owe?" he asked her.

The girl was not prepared to be put on the spot. So he asked again, "Well? How much do you owe Max for the TV, young lady?"

She pulled a number out of her head, "Five hundred dollars?" She wasn't confident in her answer.

"Five hundred dollars? Well now. That's too much for a little lady like you! Do you even have a job?" he asked.

She was starting to get more comfortable and decided to play along. "No I don't!!" she said. We laughed. He was so fun.

"Well then, why don't we just erase the books." He pretended to erase his bookkeeping. "We'll put down that you owe Max fifty dollars instead. How does that sound, hmmmm?" He looked at the girl for a response.

"Great! Thank you!" she said.

His body immediately changed back to Max, a feeble old man who had trouble getting around. He went to another girl and practically got right in her face, "Can you believe that Sly Ty giving away MY money like that? Do you know what he did after that?"

The girl said, "What?" I could tell she was glad he moved away.

He transformed quickly into the smooth talking, easy walking, Sly Ty and breezed on over to another girl, "Hey sweetie, don't you owe money to Max for a piano?"

She played along with him, "Yes!"

"And how much do YOU owe for that fine upright golden piano you bought just last month?" He raised his one eyebrow high at her.

"Um ... I don't know. One thousand dollars?" she guessed.

He gave her a hint and stuck his thumb up in the air to prompt her to raise the amount.

"Two thousand dollars?"

He raised his thumb again and exaggerated the motion so she would raise the amount a little higher. We laughed at his humor.

"Ten thousand dollars?" That was too high, so he gave her a thumbs down, and she changed her answer to $5,000. He seemed to like that.

"Well ... WELL!" he said, "Why don't we just change that number to $500. How does that sound?" He moved his hand like he was erasing the numbers and exchanging them for something lower.

The man switched into Max again and shuffled back to his seat. He looked so convincing, I thought he might fall.

Max narrated, "That Sly Ty was very shrewd. The next day I fired him, and he went back to the customers he had visited the day before."

He jumped up quickly and ran to the girls, "HELLLO!! Remember me? The guy that gave you a good deal yesterday? Turns out I need a place to stay. May I join you?"

Pretending to be immediately weak and feeble again, he became Max.

He said, "And would you believe they all welcomed him in? They gave that crook a place to live. That little slime ball."

He walked back to his stool and looked at us. "Sly Ty is really good at using what HE has to get people to welcome him into their home. But what about You? Hmmmm? You need to learn to use what YOU have so that people will welcome YOU ... into HEAVEN." He spoke slowly and exaggerated his words so that we would understand.

I thought about what Mrs. Belle said in our first lesson. I remembered how ludicrous it was that she claimed we could actually take one thing with us to heaven. She had said it was people. I was so taken back by her challenge to see people as treasure that I hadn't done anything about her claim that we could take people to heaven.

Max started to walk out, then he stopped as one does when they remember there's one more thing to say. "Oh, and that hundred dollars you've got there? That's to practice buying things for other people so that when you understand this story about Jesus, you've got some experience being generous." He exaggerated a wink and walked off.

Mrs. Belle started clapping, and we joined her. The guy who played Max, whoever he was, walked off stage.

THE CHALLENGE *by Wendy Everts*

"If you want to read that story again, you can," Mrs. Belle said. She handed out papers with *Luke 16:1-13* typed on them, so we could remember to look it up later.

"The Challenge this week is to use your money to buy things for your neighbor and to give it to them. Like Max said, the point is to practice thinking of others and being generous. We will talk more about this again next week!" She left us to go greet Max.

I was thoughtful.

I understood some things about the lesson but not all. People are treasure, and we can take them to heaven. We should use what we have to get them there, but how? Were we supposed to be like Sly Ty? That didn't seem right.

The worship team didn't come forward. Alpha Omega was just plain over, and we were left sitting next to people we didn't know very well. I left as quickly as possible and looked for Twinkle and Sara, so we could process the evening.

I had to steal my Bible back from Mom, so I could read Luke 16:1-13. I went to my room and flipped through the pages. I didn't have any idea how to find any book in the Bible, let alone Luke 16:1-13.

It would've taken me a long time to find it, except those verses had been highlighted. On the page above the verse was a sticky memo that said, *Clover, once you understand these verses, you will understand why I gave you The Challenge. God bless.*

Dinner Party

Every day Mom wore less makeup and spent less time in her wigs. It became normal to see her like she really was. If someone had told me five months ago that Mom would be comfortable in regular shoes without all the glitz, I would never have believed them. She didn't even freak out and change if a neighbor came over unexpectedly.

Now that everything was out in the open, eating dinner as a family and sharing openly about things became normal practice too.

The day Mom announced that she had invited her support group over for a dinner party, we said, "Of course you did because that's what you do now!" That would have never happened before.

After she asked me to forgive her, she stopped trying to run my life and be the perfect mom and she actually became, well ... the perfect mom. She was beautiful now in a homemade apple pie sort of way. She was comforting and felt safe.

The dinner party fell on a Friday in April, the *Use What You Have to Be Welcomed* month. Even though we didn't make T-shirts anymore, Twinkle and Sara and I still hung out every Friday night. I really wanted to see what Maggie Ann Mannerhouse was like with her support group friends. I wanted to know what they talked about and, frankly, I was curious to see what Mom would cook for them.

She worked in the kitchen all day. When I walked in the door after school, it felt like walking into Mrs. Belle's house. There were wonderful smells of food that had been carefully prepared and baked. Something was in the oven, and there were a couple of berry pies on the counter.

"Pies, Mom? I didn't know you could make pies!" I said.

"I didn't either," she said. "I've been watching cooking videos on YouTube, and I thought I would try it. Not bad, right?" She held one up for me to see, even though they were clearly visible on the counter. They were ugly, but looked really good.

"Oh, and watch this, Clovah!" She put a whole ear of corn that was still in its husk in the microwave. She pressed the button for two minutes. "I haven't tried this yet, but someone posted it on Facebook, and I can't wait to see if it works." When the oven beeped, she took the corn out and placed it on a cutting board. She cut off the stalk end and squeezed the corn from the top. It slid out of its husk without the little hairs, cooked to perfection. Mom was delighted.

"It seemed too good to be true, but it really worked!" She seemed proud and repeated the process for all fifteen ears of corn.

I helped her set the table and put out extra chairs, so we could all sit together. Everything we did seemed natural, even though we had never had anyone over for dinner before.

All the guests were expected around 6:00, and around 5:30 my brother came out of his room smelling like Axe cologne. He had obviously groomed himself with vigor.

"Whoa! What is going on? You are usually ugly. Are you getting married tonight?" I asked.

"No!" he said, and his face flushed red.

"Why are you so dressed up, Ryan?" I asked. It was a fair question.

"I'm not dressed up, Clover!" he insisted.

"Alright, alright!" I backed off.

Lisa arrived first, and I found out pretty quickly why my brother was "not dressed up." Lisa was wearing makeup and also had on her best clothes.

"Lisa! You look so cute," I said. I was really impressed.

"Thank you, Clover." She was distracted by something to my left. "Hey, Ryan, how are you?"

"Good," my brother said. He shifted around nervously like he had never talked to a girl before.

Thank goodness another person knocked right then, so we could have a hormone break. I went to the door, and Lisa went to sit down with Ryan.

One by one, folks showed up. Dad came home from work and slipped into his Friday night comfy clothes. We all gathered around the table and Dad prayed. Even though Dad and Mom prayed before dinner with us, it still felt new to hear them do it.

Tackling dinner with guests over was a new experience for me. It was just eating, but having other people there made me feel like I didn't know how to do it. Should I start eating when I put food on my plate? Or did I have to wait until everyone got their food? Would anyone care if I put my elbows on the table?

Mom took the brisket out of the oven and set it on the table like a beautiful centerpiece. All the girls went nuts. They knew each other so well and weren't inhibited in any way.

"My stars, Maggie Ann, this smells so great! I think I'm gonna stick my whole face in it!" one of them said in a raspy loud voice.

"Yeah, no kidding. It's almost too bad we aren't all in chemo anymore, so we could taste it twice! Am I right?" They all laughed like it was perfectly alright to talk about barfing right before eating.

Our house had turned into a rowdy night club, which was a welcome change from the monotonous meals we used to have.

I tasted two things that night: Mom's good food, and the way to entertain company. I had lived so long without experiencing the feeling of deep friendship around the table, and I really liked it. Not that they were my friends personally, but I felt like they knew me. They had shared something with Mom and had helped her open up in a way that completely changed her.

When dinner was over and we all settled into conversation around the table, I heard Lisa say to my brother, "Wanna get some fresh air with me?"

"Sure," he said. They stepped away from the table and went outside.

We had all collectively paid attention to their exit and tried not to make a big deal about it until they had shut the door. I let loose like a water hose.

"What just happened there? Did my brother walk outside alone with a girl? I hope he doesn't chop her up with all that Axe cologne he's wearing," I teased.

Mom said, "Shhhh! Clovah! She's going to ask him to the Under Classy Dance."

"What? You know about this? That's not even right, Mom. Did you ALL know about this?" They smiled and nodded and clapped tiny quiet claps.

I interrupted their cheering, "And why are we being quiet again? They are outside."

"Because they could come back any minute, and we don't want it to be awkward," Mom said.

"Like it's not going to be awkward already when they walk back in? What's an Under Classy Dance?" I asked.

"It's really fun," said one of the ladies. I was glad she wasn't whispering. "It's the same night as the prom, except it's for the freshmen and sophomores. Thus, UNDER CLASSy dance, get it? It's a girl-ask-guy square dance at the Jenkins' barn. They get a caller and they teach you real line dancing and other hoedown dances."

"And all you can eat bacon, don't forget that," the one with the raspy voice said. "That's what gets the boys there.

Another woman piped up, "Actually a team of students from Alpha Omega started it. They were really disappointed that kids were drinking and not dancing on prom night, so they thought they would do something about it. Now, instead of kids hanging out on the edge of the dance floor and getting into trouble at the prom, they are all line dancing and even using hoedown moves that they learned from the Under Classy Dance."

I tried to imagine my brother line dancing with Lisa at the Under Classy Dance. That was a stretch.

Lisa and Ryan stayed outside a long time. Long enough for us to forget that they were even out there. When they came back in, most people had left. Ryan went straight to his room after he said goodbye to Lisa. I stuck my mouth into the corner of my brother's closed door and said, "Hey Ryan, did you need me to put your shirt in the wash from all the drool you just got all over it?"

"Yes, Clover, I do," he said, calm and sarcastic. Not the answer I was expecting, which shut down my teasing immediately. Maybe he had learned a thing or two from Twinkle.

I went to bed and thought about my graduation from middle school in one month and what high school and dancing with boys next year would be like. It sure felt different to think about growing up under parents who had friends and no secrets.

I was ready.

Business Suit
Jesus

I repossessed my Bible from Mom, and every night I took it out and read the highlighted verses again and again. I hoped I would find some clue about how to use what I have so that people would welcome me into heaven. After reading Luke 16:1-13 over and over again, I realized that until Mrs. Belle explained it to me, there was no chance of understanding.

On the bus, I grilled Sara and Twinkle about every little thing I was reading. I even brought my Bible to school in my backpack.

"Listen to what this says," I read to them, "Verse nine, *And I tell you, make friends for yourselves by means of unrighteous wealth, so that when it fails they may receive you into the eternal dwellings.*

"Doesn't that sound like the story Max acted out? Like we are supposed to be like that creepy guy that made friends so we can mooch off them? Isn't that using them? How can using people even be a Christian idea? It's like buying friends."

"Jesus said that we USE unrighteous wealth," Twinkle responded. "He didn't say the goal was unrighteous or that WE are supposed to be unrighteous."

"Isn't it though? Am I the only one who is struggling here? Tell me you guys think the goal seems unrighteous." I really wondered why they weren't questioning like I was.

"I think the goal is to have people greet me in heaven. Having people that I know in heaven doesn't sound unrighteous. It sounds awesome. I wonder what it would take to use what I have so that Nat and Audrey could welcome me into heaven," Twinkle pondered.

That distracted me. The whole subject of Audrey was a sore spot in my heart. I got back on subject. "Then what does it mean that money is unrighteous? And ... what does unrighteous even MEAN?"

Twinkle totally bypassed my question and went on with her own previous thought. "Think about Nat and Audrey. Who knows what they understand about God. Especially Nat. What if when you entered heaven, she was there to welcome you?"

I looked straight ahead, but I wasn't looking at the bus seat in front of me. I was trying to picture Nat in heaven giving me a high five and a hug as I walked toward the presence of God. Heck, I was just trying to imagine her doing that in the lunchroom.

"Yeah, that's a totally cool picture, Twinkle, but how is that connected with unrighteous money?" She needed some help to focus on my question.

"I don't know, but when I understand, I'll do whatever it takes. Because if Jesus said it, then it must work, and I'm doing it." Twinkle resolved.

Sara decided to jump in, "I'm doing it too. I want to see Nat take a ring."

"I don't know yet if I'm in. I need more time," I said bravely.

I fell silent, wondering.

"What are you thinking about, Clover?" asked Sara. She was always so good at listening to me.

"I'm thinking about Jesus. I used to picture him as such a weak hippie guy before I came to Alpha Omega."

"And now?" Sara asked.

"Now, I don't know. He's taken off his hippie flower power shirt and exchanged it for either a corrupt business suit or ...."

"Or what?" she pressed me.

"I don't know. I haven't decided if he is corrupt or brilliant," I confessed.

Sara smiled, "I think he's brilliant!"

A Giant Welcome

*W*hen we walked into Alpha Omega, there were pieces of paper sitting on our chairs, and I doodled on mine right away.

"Clover, what are you doing? You don't even know what those are for yet!" Twinkle was such a rule follower.

"I know, but I've decided not to worry about that." I doodled on.

"What if we have to share something personal and then pass it to someone we don't know? Yours is going to have a silly face on it. Everyone is going to know you are a bad drawer!"

"HEY!!!" I tried to be offended, but she was right. "Well, shoot." I grabbed Twinkle's paper before she knew what happened and threw mine on the floor, so she would have to pick it up and use it as her own. "Now people will think you are a bad drawer! Ha!"

"Clover! Give it back!" She reached over to grab it, and I shoved it down my shirt. Her eyes got wide and she started laughing. "Oh. My. GOSH. Clover!" She picked up my paper and started drawing on it. Now I got worried.

When she was done, I grabbed it again and threw her blank one on the ground. She had bested me. She had lured me in, and I wanted it back.

On the paper she wrote, "Tell my dad I need B.A. medicine," in a thought bubble by the head I had drawn.

I chuckled and stuck it down my shirt to signify that the battle was over. As I looked at her, I said, "Shrewd and clever girl!" The worship team started up the meeting. It was nice to horse around and have friends who knew me.

We sang just one song. That usually meant the activity would be longer, which I was glad for. Hopefully Mrs. Belle would explain everything. I was counting on it.

I noticed that behind the worship team there were some long tables with a bunch of stuff hidden on them. The last time there were props off to the side, I had bawled all evening. I hoped this wasn't a crying night.

Finally, Lisa came up front. Great. Last time the ninth graders were in charge, it was a sob fest.

She told us to write the person's name who was responsible for getting us to come to Alpha Omega on our paper. That was easy. I took my paper out from my shirt and wrote, *Mom*.

I reminisced back to the day we drove into Hitlery and to our house for the first time. I remembered Mom had said, "I signed you up for a club Clovah!" How different I felt now. So much had changed in a year.

Lisa also asked us to write down the name of the person who had influenced us the most in our relationship with Christ. "This one will take a little bit more time," Lisa said. "Who has invested in you, and what have they done? How have they spent their time and their money on you?" She was reading her questions from a piece of paper so that she could remember everything.

I immediately remembered what Mrs. Belle had said to me in her backyard. *"The purpose of The Challenge was to woo you to Jesus, Clover."*

I wrote: Mrs. Belle, $1,000, and a challenge. Everyone was still busy writing, so I thought a little harder in case I was missing something.

Mom's support group came to mind. If it weren't for them, the deal I had made with God to show me the truth about Mom's wig wouldn't have happened. Mrs. Belle took the time to prepare the talks for Alpha Omega ...

Suddenly my mind was flooded with memories of how people had invested in me this year. Sara had walked with me every day and had listened to me for hours on end. Mrs. Belle had given me a job walking the dog, so I could apply the talks I heard every week. Even before that, when Dad got the job at the shopping network, Mrs. Belle had helped Mom get acquainted with Hitlery before we even moved here. And Twinkle had told me I was treasure.

Lisa's voice pulled me back from memory lane. "What did you guys write on your paper? How have people invested in you?"

The room was quiet for a while. Lisa said, "If someone doesn't share first, I am going to start calling on people!" She had a nervous laugh.

The room was still quiet. "Okay, okay! I'll start." Lisa broke the silence. "You guys all know that Mrs. Belle gave me $1,000 toward the fundraiser," she said, "Not to mention all the sweet notes she wrote me and the hours of listening."

I was thankful she didn't point me out too.

Someone else got brave, "Okay I'll go. One of the volunteers took me out for ice cream after I'd been coming for a couple weeks to ask what I was thinking about after those first talks."

"Yeah," said another girl, "A volunteer called and invited me to a small group. She made us homemade cookies every time.

She found out what our favorite things were, and she surprised us with them."

That reminded me of The Challenge this last week. I was supposed to buy Nike socks, Converse high tops, and a Build-a-Bear for that girl. I had forgotten to do it.

Twinkle piped up next. "When I lived in Colorado, we had a family friend who was also a teacher. She wrote me notes at the beginning of the day and had them waiting for me in some of my classes. She would encourage me with scripture."

She looked sad. Maybe other people didn't notice, but Sara and I knew the story behind that family friend.

Lisa shared again, "All these things brought us to know Jesus. People used what they had to invest in us. They used their 'unrighteous wealth' so that we could welcome them into heaven."

I was listening. I trusted Lisa. Certainly what everyone did for me this year didn't feel like Sly Ty. I knew that Mrs. Belle loved me.

"Let me give you a visual of what this looks like." She read from verse nine, the same verse I read over and over at home and on the bus. "And I tell you, make friends for yourselves by means of unrighteous wealth, so that when it fails they may receive you into the eternal dwellings."

All the ninth grade girls came up. "I bet most of you are here because of Mrs. Belle," Lisa said. "Maybe even some of you took a ring and began a relationship with Jesus because of her."

I pulled the necklace out of my shirt and played with the ring that was on it. Mrs. Belle had done so much for me. She loved me. I was starting to get it.

"We invited a few 'friends' that Mrs. Belle has made with 'unrighteous wealth.'" Lisa motioned that it was time for others to come in.

People started pouring in. My mom and dad came in with a lot of people I recognized from their vow ceremony. Tons of high school kids that I didn't recognize. There were about fifty altogether.

Lisa gathered the crowd up front and said, "Mrs. Belle has no idea what we are doing tonight. The ninth graders kicked her out. We told her to wait in the library until one of us came to get her." They all looked excited.

Lisa lifted her hand to the crowd, "MANY of us wouldn't know Jesus right now if it weren't for Mrs. Belle. All of us will welcome her into heaven. Tonight we wanted to give her a taste of what that is going to be like."

The worship team started singing a song that we all knew. We were invited to sing along as they played.

The whole group got into a line by the door. A couple people went to the tables and lifted the sheets. There was a feast of refreshments and drinks. Balloons popped up that had been held down by the weight of the sheets. A couple girls brought in a huge piece of butcher paper that they quickly stuck on the back wall by the food. It said, "We will welcome you in heaven. THANK YOU!"

"Let her in!!" Lisa said excitedly. The whole group started clapping in rhythm as the worship team played a celebratory song.

We stood up to see.

Mrs. Belle walked through the door, and the whole crowd of people lifted their hands and cheered for her. She stopped and put her hands to her face. I could tell she was surprised. Each person in line hugged her and welcomed her into the room.

As each person in line finished greeting her, they went to the back wall and put their picture on the butcher paper. It took a long time. We watched and sang.

That Lisa really knew how to plan a sob-fest.

The back wall filled up with pictures of people who would welcome Mrs. Belle in heaven, and the singing became louder as those who had hugged Mrs. Belle came to wait and sing along with us.

Once everything was done, the worship team stopped and the room was awkwardly quiet. Someone yelled, "Speech, speech!" And we all joined in. We wanted to know what she would say after that.

For the first time, Mrs. Belle looked like she didn't know what to say.

She took her time and embraced the moment. "Wow … if that's how it feels on Earth, imagine what Heaven will be like."

She took another moment. She used the opportunity to inspire us. "Who will welcome you?" she asked. "Who will be in heaven because of you? How will you use 'unrighteous wealth' to gain friends? You won't know how to do it right away. You will have to practice. But try. Do something!" That reminded me of what Sara had said to me the morning we were walking. She was definitely her granddaughter.

That was a powerful night for me.

I thought of the sticky note Mrs. Belle had stuck in my Bible by the highlighted verses. It said that I would understand The Challenge more after this month's theme. I did understand. She wanted me to welcome her too.

If they did this again, I would join my parents in the crowd and put my picture on the wall.

I thought about her question, 'Who would be in heaven because of me?' Wasn't that what Sara and Twinkle had said on the bus? They wanted to see Nat and Audrey there.

Oh dear … Audrey. There was a little something I needed to take care of before I used my 'unrighteous wealth' to woo her into a relationship with Jesus.

New Chapter

It was time to confess to Audrey that I was, indeed, the one who had drawn the picture of her giant mouth in history class.

I didn't confess because I had to. I didn't do it because I wanted to. I did it because every day that I spent time with Audrey and Nat seemed like a lie. Time was not healing, time was revealing. Talking to Audrey and Nat would be my only way out, even if it meant risking our friendship.

I waited until the last month of school. If they didn't want to forgive me, and I had to go back to my old lunch table, at least there wouldn't be much of the school year left. I chose to tell them on a Friday. That way I would have the whole weekend to sulk if it went badly.

We sat at our usual lunch table, and I didn't even have to break the news. I was unusually quiet, and they noticed that.

"Okay, what's wrong, Clover? You've been sad and quiet all day," Audrey said.

"Yes, something is wrong, but I'm scared to say it because when I say it, everything might change." I prepared them for my confession.

Twinkle clammed up immediately. She could tell what I was about to do. She gave me a knowing look of sympathy.

"Oh, Clover, don't tell us you are moving!" Nat said in a mad tone. My heart sank. She actually really did like me, which made what I was about to say even more risky. My hands got clammy, and I felt sick.

"It's okay if you don't want to sit with me anymore after I tell you this. I get it if you don't ever want to talk to me again." I looked at Nat, "Whatever names you are about to call me, I totally deserve it." My voice had the shaky wavering quality of someone about to cry.

Nat became a wall of protection. She acted like she didn't care, but I could tell that she did. Audrey, on the other hand, kept eating her sandwich like we were about to talk about puppies.

There was no easy way to do this, so I just blurted it out. "I was the one that drew the picture of you with the big mouth in history class, Audrey." Twinkle put her arm around me.

"I can't live with myself anymore. I need you to know so that maybe you will forgive me." I was looking down at my lap and didn't even see the explosion that was about to happen from Nat.

"That was YOU, Clover?" A look of hatred took over her face.

"You are such a two-faced liar!" Nat shouted. "I can't believe you did that. You go to church and pretend you're all perfect. You sit with us and pretend that you like us, but then you go behind our backs and ...." She didn't finish that sentence. She was too mad.

"You are such a faker," she continued. "I was starting to trust that there were actually people in the world that were good, but you're just like my dad after all. Maybe everyone is. Maybe the world really does completely suck." I could tell she was starting to cry but was willing herself to hold it in. She got up and said one more thing before she left.

THE CHALLENGE *by Wendy Everts*

"You and your Jesus can move far away and never come back!"

I covered my face while she was talking, but that didn't protect me. No one had ever said words like that to me before. It felt dark, ugly. I didn't feel better. I felt worse.

When I looked up, Sara was gone. Of course. I had forgotten that she didn't know either, only Twinkle. I had forgotten that this could ruin my friendship with her too. Oh misery! How could I have done that to Sara? I should've told her in person first! If Nat and Audrey never talked with me again that was one thing, but Sara?

"Where's Sara?" I asked.

Audrey answered, "She got up after Nat started yelling. The whole lunchroom was staring at us. They kind of still are."

Looking around the room, I could see that she was right. Embarrassed, I turned away and focused back on our table. Audrey was calmly eating her sandwich.

"Audrey," I said. "Are you okay? You don't even seem surprised."

"Oh I already knew you did it, Clover," she said.

That took a second to really sink in.

"WHAT?!?!" Twinkle said.

"You knew? How did you know?" I asked.

"Yeah, I knew. When I was venting with you at the table after it happened, Twinkle described who she thought did it and said that it might be a girl. I figured it might be a cheerleader, but you weren't acting like yourself. I didn't KNOW know it was you, but I dealt with the fact that you could've done it a long time ago. Don't worry, I'm used to people doing stuff like that to me, so I'm over it. I've been over it for a while."

I wasn't sure what to say next. "It makes me sad that you are used to it. You deserve better than that, Audrey. I never thought that I would stoop to that level. You are one of my best friends! And I DID! I did do it!" I told her exactly what she meant to me, exactly how I really felt.

"Thanks for admitting it. It's good to know you did it. It's nice not to have to wonder anymore." She was stoic.

What was happening? Audrey was a wall. She was way stronger than I thought she was. It was Nat and Sara who were going to be tricky. What would I do if Audrey forgave me, but not Sara and Nat? Would we all split up? I hadn't even thought that far. I never thought we could be divided. I just thought that everyone would either accept me, or everyone would hate me.

And then there was the bus stop. How could I stand at the bus stop all alone with Sara now? I wouldn't do it. I would ride my bike five miles to school every day if I had to. Or I could ask Mom to drive me, but there was no way that would work. We lived too far from school. I would have to face Sara.

"Well," I said to Twinkle and Audrey, "I sort of blew things up a bit. Maybe I shouldn't have said a word if you already knew. Maybe this could've been ...." Audrey was crying. We were sitting next to each other, so I didn't notice until I looked over at her.

"Oh, Audrey!" My heart melted to see her so fragile. I put my arm around her.

She whispered, "No one has ever said I was one of their best friends before." She pulled back and looked at me. Her eyes were wet. "I'm sorry. I tried to play it cool, so you wouldn't know how much that meant to me. I guess this is what it feels like to have someone apologize to you. I feel better, thank you."

Just then someone came by our table and ruined the meaningful moment by throwing a piece of paper on the table. "Here, someone told me to give this to you."

I read the note aloud. "Wasn't sure if I needed a glucose pill or a good cry. I am okay. You did the right thing. See you on the bus." It wasn't signed, but I knew it was from Sara.

I felt relief like never before. Sara said that I had done the right thing. I would keep that note forever. I rested my head on my hands and propped it up with my elbows. My head felt like a huge boulder that I couldn't hold up all by myself.

"Nat is coming over to my house tonight," Audrey said. "Maybe she will talk with me, maybe she won't. Usually when she's mad she sticks to herself. We'll see." Audrey was very matter-of-fact. She wasn't worried. Why should she be? Nat wasn't mad at HER!

"I feel better, and I don't feel better," I said. The lunch bell rang, and we were off to see if time could heal. If Nat was lost forever, then it would be all my fault. At least, it felt that way.

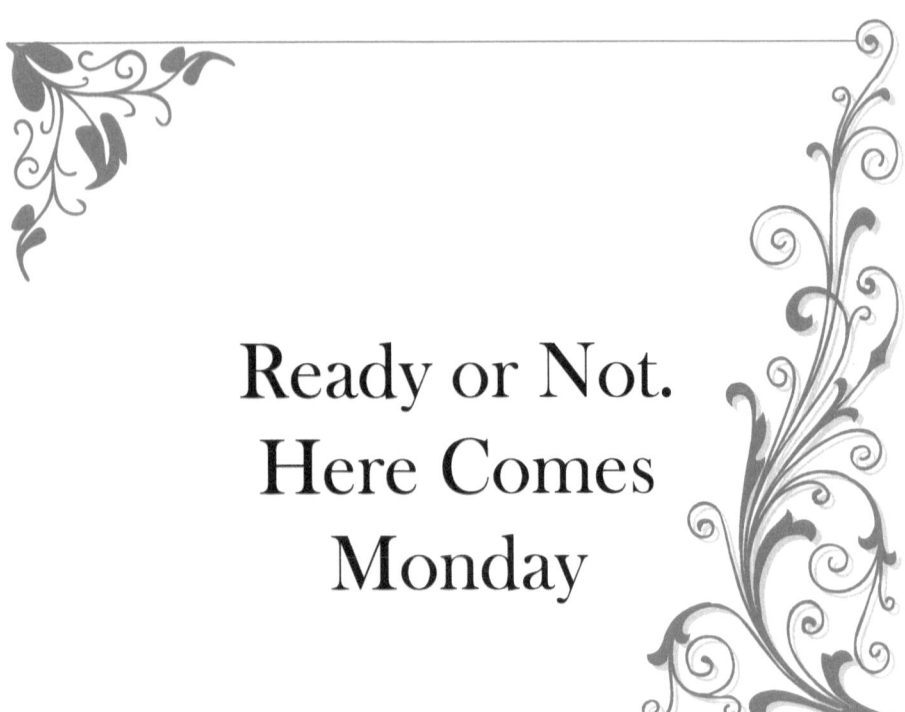

Ready or Not.
Here Comes
Monday

*S*o now what? There was part of me that was crying out and angry that we all didn't end with a big hug.

Twinkle was my new hero. Her experience with their family friend had taught me that being a Christian wasn't all roses. In a way, I was prepared for the worst. I knew life could be like this.

Twinkle said something interesting when we hung out that night after my big confession. She said that even though Nat stomped off with bad words toward Jesus, at least she'd experienced someone who told the truth and said they were sorry. Twinkle said I showed her what Christianity was all about. People who don't understand mercy can't give it.

I couldn't expect Nat to forgive me.

Nat wasn't at school on Monday, and when she came back, she acted as though we had never been friends. I didn't have to worry about the lunch table situation because Nat never even came into the lunchroom, at least that I could see. I couldn't stand being at the same school with her, knowing that she hated me.

Is that how life was going to be now? I leaned on Twinkle. She knew what it was like to have life feel sour with no assurance that it would get better. Every day she lived with the fact that their family friend wouldn't speak to them anymore. Maybe we don't always get the change we crave but, instead, get the perspective we need to see something from God's point of view.

The last few weeks of English class were so needed. Our end-of-the-year essay gave me a way to put all my thoughts and feelings down on paper. If everything couldn't be wrapped up with a neat bow, at least I could see the gifts from this year that I had in my box.

If our final essay assignment hadn't been to use ironic statements and similes, I would never have processed everything so thoroughly.

I reread all my similes and ironic statements that I'd collected all year, which were mostly about Alpha Omega and Mrs. Belle. I looked through my scrapbook that my Secret Santa had started. There were pictures of me when we first moved here and pictures of Mom. Pictures of her ridiculous high heels and wigs. I had forgotten how thick her makeup had been, and I forgot that I had never seen her without it. I forgot what it was like to be in a family that had secrets and never talked about a thing. There were pictures of the vow ceremony, and there were pictures of Mom taking her wig off for the first time in public.

I sat at my desk to write. I turned on my fuzzy troll doll lamp and smiled. That lamp had become a comfort to me. I hardly ever used it, but it seemed fitting to turn it on while writing an essay about my year.

I plugged away at writing, while spending most of my time staring at the wall. Writing was hard, and there were moments I just didn't know how to end the thing. I stared at the wall and noticed a little flake of white on the paint. Then I really started looking and saw other flakes of white in the same area.

I rubbed my hand over the space to wipe away the flakes. The wall was bumpy under my fingers. I turned the lamp and shined it directly on the area. From a certain angle, I could see that someone had written on the wall in white crayon. It was practically impossible to see.

I took my pencil and very faintly traced over the area to expose the white crayon. It was some sort of message. I stepped back, squinted my eyes, and made out some words that said: *Treasure Front Yard*.

Did that mean there was treasure in the front yard? I thought I would go check.

Where would it be? How do you start looking for treasure? The yard was rocky and had patches of plants that didn't need much water. The Matilija poppies that nuzzled up against the house caught my eye. I looked for something that would give me a clue about buried treasure.

I lifted up a poppy branch and saw a rock that had writing on it. It said, "Matthew 6:21." I ran to get my Bible. Maybe that was a clue.

The table of contents led me to Matthew, and I finally found the verse, but it took me a long time. There it was, Matthew 6:21 *For where your treasure is, there your heart will be also*. That was our theme in Alpha Omega this year.

I hated puzzles. Just to make sure I wasn't missing the obvious, I started digging under the rock. Sure enough, I found a plain shoebox that had *Treasure Capsule* written on the top.

I was invigorated. I imagined finding gold and fine diamonds inside. But at first glance, I could tell that this was something far more personal. There was a note lying on top of the contents of the box.

> *If you find this, then you are living in my house. There is a girl two doors down, and she is THE bestest friend*

a girl could ever have. I don't want to leave her, but my parents are making me go.

This is a box of our friendship that I would like to keep buried here please. It's a part of me that can stay. Feel free to look at it.

If you ever meet Sara, tell her that I love her and that I miss her every day.

Love, Bethany

What do you do after reading a letter like that? Salty tears had already reached my lips, and I could taste the sadness.

Underneath were pictures of Bethany and Sara, who had played together since they were babies. There were lockets and ticket stubs and notes they had written each other. I read each one.

I held the box and was so thankful. I was thankful that I found it and thankful that I got to meet Bethany and see her love for Sara. It was the same love I had for Sara too. I buried the box and went back inside to finish my essay.

I wrote and wrote until the only thing left for my essay was the title. I thought about the rock that led me to the treasure capsule, and it became clear what my essay was about. My year had been filled with the same treasure.

I titled my essay just like that rock that led to me to Bethany's treasure:

Matthew 6:21.

Disneyland

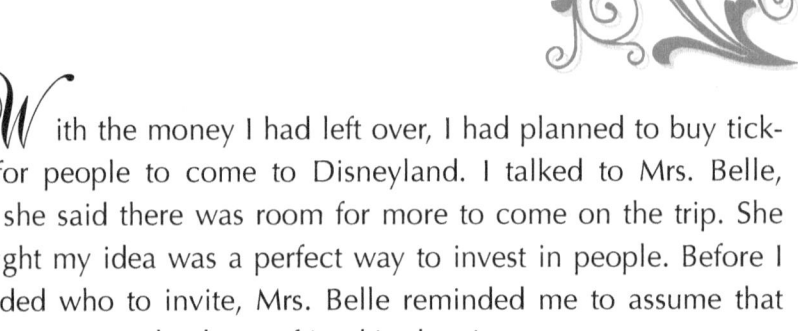

ith the money I had left over, I had planned to buy tickets for people to come to Disneyland. I talked to Mrs. Belle, and she said there was room for more to come on the trip. She thought my idea was a perfect way to invest in people. Before I decided who to invite, Mrs. Belle reminded me to assume that everyone wanted to be my friend in due time.

Audrey was very excited when I invited her, and as you can probably guess, Nat never called me back. I left a message to let her know I wanted her to come. Mrs. Belle's words had inspired me to reach out to her.

Twinkle, Audrey, Sara, and I had a blast at Disneyland. I bought us Mickey Mouse ears, and we tried to take pictures of random boys without them seeing us.

After the trip, Mrs. Belle pulled us aside and asked if we would be ninth grade helpers for Alpha Omega next year. She told Audrey that, even though she hadn't been a part of the group this year, she could still do it as long as Sara, Twinkle, and I said yes.

Before Audrey could say anything, Mrs. Belle handed her a familiar envelope. I knew what had to be inside.

My heart softened toward Audrey as I thought about the year ahead of her. Her challenge would be different than mine. I remembered how Lisa had reacted when I showed her my challenge. She didn't say a word. Until now, I didn't understand why.

"Oh Audrey, I got that same envelope last year. I don't know what to say. Just open it and see what happens."

About the author

*I*n my middle school years, I had a youth director who took me under her wing. She saw that my dad was suffering from Paranoid Schizophrenia, and my parents were getting a divorce. My youth director invested in me, gave me a listening ear, and taught me about the person of Jesus Christ.

In college I became a member of InterVarsity Christian Fellowship, where numerous mentors invested in me. I experienced healing and transformation and peace.

It is no surprise that I have a deep interest in giving others what my mentors gave me. I help people come out of hiding and experience the freedom of transparency, encounter Jesus in scripture, and be changed by him. I teach people how to study scripture, apply it, and grow.

This book is meant not only to entertain, but to equip and enable folks to disciple others, to understand and share the gospel, and to give a picture of true transformation and becoming free from the past. This is not a story based on my life only, but the hundreds of lives that I have had the joy of being a part of.

It's a testimony of the change that can happen in all of us. The church really can create space for God to grab us, change us, mold us, and make us new.

Wendy Everts

A special private thanks

$\mathcal{T}$he second point in *The Challenge* is to give in secret and I honor that here.

To my editors, readers, financial supporters, emotional cheerleaders, and web designers, you know who you are. THANK YOU!!!!
    You have fully accomplished Challenge #8, as well. May you get MANY high fives!

~ Wendy Everts